GUNS OF JUSTICE

Staffordshire Library and Information Services
Please return or renew by the last date shown

A   e
ke   r
of   y
fiv   f
Sh   e
ho   .
W   d
ev   .
Fo   f
Se   y
M   ,
an   a
ha

If not required by other readers, this item may may be renewed in person, by post or telephone, online or by email. To renew, either the book or ticket are required

24 Hour Renewal Line
0845 33 00 740

Staffordshire
County Council

GUNS OF JUSTICE

by

Hal Jons

Dales Large Print Books
Long Preston, North Yorkshire,
BD23 4ND, England.

British Library Cataloguing in Publication Data.

Jons, Hal
    Guns of justice.

A catalogue record of this book is
available from the British Library

ISBN   978-1-84262-888-1 pbk

First published in Great Britain in 1980 by Robert Hale Ltd.

Published in Large Print 2012 by arrangement with
Hal Jons, care of Mrs M. Kneller

Dales Large Print is an imprint of Library Magna Books Ltd.

Printed and bound in Great Britain by
T.J. (International) Ltd., Cornwall, PL28 8RW

Chapter One

Mallory eased away from the swing-doors of the Maverick saloon and leaned against the sidewalk rail as folk along the length of Main Street rushed to question the riders entering town from the north. As they emerged out of the ruck of people the five riders headed for the saloon; the sixth, draped over a saddle, would never enjoy another drink. It was Suter's body that excited most comment however, and the crowd milled behind, eager to know what happened.

At the hitchrail the riders dismounted and made desultory attempts to brush the dust out of their clothing.

'What happened to Suter? and what about Willard?' It was Con Lacey, the blacksmith, who asked the question.

Manning glanced impatiently at the saloon before answering. 'We got jumped by Willard and he got away with our broncs after plugging Suter.'

'Did Suter call his hand?' Lacey asked. Manning shrugged and glanced towards Dainton and Nolan, who stood close together.

'No – I guess young Des didn't give Suter

any chance at all.' Dainton's voice dripped sorrow. 'He killed the sheriff in cold blood just so that we'd be persuaded to do what he said *muy pronto.*'

Mallory moved behind a couple of punchers as Manning, Dainton and Nolan pushed their way into the saloon, then as Tyler and Creasey led the horse bearing the corpse to the funeral parlour, he made his way along the sidewalk to Doc Colehan's house on the edge of town. The second knock brought the cherubic, easy-going doctor to the door and his smile was one of real pleasure and welcome.

'Hiya, Jack – come on inside.' Then as Mallory followed him into the big, neat dining-room. 'You just visiting or wanting my professional advice?' The Doc's hand was hovering over a bottle of bourbon as he spoke, and Mallory smiled. It was a known fact that the Doc never mixed business with pleasure.

'I guess I'm in pretty good shape, Doc,' he replied, then held out his hand for the glass Colehan had filled for him.

'What's your problem, then?' Doc settled his bulk on the edge of his big maple-wood table and surveyed the younger man blandly.

'The problem's Des Willard, or rather what might happen to him unless some folk get around to clearing his name.'

'I suppose it's natural that you'd want to

side him, Jack, considering you've been pards from way back, but the way I heard it the evidence is pretty solid against him. I reckon Jeff didn't rate very high with most folk but that don't mean to say they're ready to let his killer go free.'

Jack Mallory took a sip of bourbon and rolled it around his tongue a few times before replying. 'Do you think Des could kill anyone in cold blood from behind, Doc?'

'If he did, and mind you it looks that way, then I'm not as good a judge of character as I thought.'

'Well, the hombres who want Des Willard to swing are going to get powerful support now. Suter's body was just brought in and Willard's supposed to have killed him in cold blood.'

'I heard the ruckus a few minutes ago.' Doc Colehan was thoughtful, 'Five men went along with Suter on Willard's trail, so if they say Des did the killing, then I guess that's how it was. I'm sure sorry Suter's got himself killed though, he was a mighty good lawman.'

'Yeah – Suter was all right, but things are not like they seem. I saw Suter lying with two wounds in his hide and got the story from Manning and Dainton. Then I caught up with Des, who'd taken their cayuses. He said he'd fired one shot and I checked his

9

guns. There was only one chamber empty. The shot Des fired creased Suter's skull, the shot that killed the sheriff was plumb through the heart.'

There was a long period of silence during which the Doc poured out a couple more glasses of bourbon. 'You're not going to get any luck with that story, Jack. I guess the words of five witnesses will be enough to make Willard pay the penalty.'

'I'm not going to spread the story, Doc. I'm hoping to whittle away at the men who are lined up against Des until somebody breaks. Just one thing, though: if you're going to examine Suter's body at the funeral parlour I'd rather you didn't dig for the slug that killed him; there might be a better time to bring it to light.'

Doc Colehan shrugged his burly shoulders. 'I shall not be probing Suter's corpse,' he declared. 'But take care, Jack, a lot of good men have died before today fighting for the wrong cause. Just be sure that Willard is innocent before you stick your neck out too far.'

Jack Mallory stood up and nodded grimly. 'I'll take care, Doc.'

As Colehan watched the younger man make his way out of the house a worried frown creased his forehead. He knew Mallory, and was concerned for his future. He knew that, once committed to a course,

10

Mallory would follow it to the bitter end. Colehan reckoned he had trouble enough making his horse ranch pay.

Jack Mallory retraced his steps along the sidewalk to the Maverick saloon and, pushing through the doors, made his way to the bar. The five central figures turned as they saw his reflection in the big glass mirror and there was bitterness on every face. Mallory ignored them and eased to the bar alongside Slim Manning. Con Sullivan the barkeep cocked an eye at him and Mallory nodded for his usual tipple. He preferred rye.

'That was mighty unfriendly of you, Mallory, not collecting cayuses for us,' Slim Manning said in a level voice. Mallory half turned and stared at the lawman.

'You could walk to hell and gone for all I care,' he replied. 'It just happens, though, that I brought your cayuses back; they're in the livery running up a feed bill for you. That is except Dainton's Paint; I guess Willard's riding that one on account Dainton never paid for it.'

Dainton shot an aggrieved look at the younger man but with admirable restraint said nothing. The deputy was low on restraint and lost no time in aggravating the situation.

'Willard's a murderer an' I reckon he's a liar too if he says he never got paid for that paint-horse, I never knew Dainton to shy on

11

a payment, so I guess he's a horse-thief too. Did you get to talking to him?'

'That's my affair,' Mallory said brusquely.

'That's not so! He's a killer on the run and if you talked and hold back information about the direction he's heading, then you're siding him.' There was a cold gleam in Manning's eyes as he spoke, and Tyler, Nolan and Creasey grinned widely in appreciation. 'I've got a durned good mind to slap you in the hoosegow until you tell me what happened when you met up.'

Mallory eased away from the bar a little and turned to face the lawman. The good-humour lines had vanished from his face and his big, dark blue eyes were steady as they probed Manning's face.

'You'll need a lot of help, Manning,' he murmured. 'A lot more help than you've got beside you right now.'

Dainton's restraining hand was on the lawman's arm as Mallory's words sunk home and he butted in before the lawman could take action.

'What grouch is eating you, Mallory? We all know you and Des Willard were mighty close pards but that don't give you the right to side him now he's turned killer, leastways not in Butane County.'

The horse-rancher turned to the bar and tossed down his drink, then paused in front of Dainton before going out. 'It's my opinion,

12

Dainton, that Willard never killed anyone.'

With Mallory's back framed briefly in the doorway as the batwing doors swung open, Dainton's hand closed like a vice on Manning's wrist as the lawman made to draw.

'Let him go,' he hissed. 'He can talk all he wants, it cuts no ice. We've got Willard to rights and nothing Mallory says can alter it.'

Jack Mallory paused a moment on the sidewalk outside the saloon. He knew he should seek out Sheila Scott, the banker's daughter, to let her know that Des Willard was safe and to set her mind at rest against the belief that Des was a killer, but he fought shy of the meeting. Although the three of them had been friends as children, Mallory had found reserve building up inside himself as the years developed Sheila into womanhood, and he no longer felt easy in her company. The reason he understood well enough, he was very much in love with her, had been in fact all the time, but no doubt some prescience had warned him that she was the natural partner for Des Willard, and the belief had built up a wall of diffidence.

Any decision was taken from him. As he stared moodily across the street the girl came out of Frank Hamer's store carrying a couple of parcels. She saw Mallory and waving a greeting, waited in front of the store for him to join her. A shaft of sunlight from between two buildings spotlighted her dark beauty as he crossed the street. The neat gingham dress she wore clung to her lithe form and he felt the usual constriction affecting his vocal chords. Her big, limpid, brown eyes were sad as she greeted him and a frown of concern creased her normally smooth forehead. She held out her hand in an impulsive movement, then withdrew it as she saw the stiffening of Mallory's features.

'Hello, Jack.' Her voice had always held music for him but there was a flatness to her tone that he thought he understood.

'Uh – hello, Sheila, I – I'll take those parcels and walk along with you.' He felt tongue-tied and it sounded like someone else speaking.

She handed the parcels to him and they walked slowly along the sidewalk towards her house just beyond Doc Colehan's. No words were exchanged until they arrived at the gate. Mallory felt his pulse rate increasing every time his glance encompassed the girl's cool beauty, and he had to fight hard to keep his loyalty to Des Willard, while Sheila thought she had never seen Mallory look more handsome and virile. He was about to hand her parcels back when she spoke with infinite sadness.

'What's to happen to Des now, Jack?' It took a long time for Mallory to look into her face. It was hard knowing those wide, smooth lips would never be for him.

'Nothing if I can help it, Sheila,' he said

14

simply. 'I don't think Des is a killer and maybe with luck he'll be cleared.'

Mallory felt the intensity of the girl's stare.

'How can you say that, Jack? – I didn't believe he could have killed Jeff, but I just heard that Manning, Dainton and some others saw him kill the sheriff. Heaven knows. I don't want him to be guilty but they can't all be wrong.'

'Maybe they can. Anyway, Des says so and I guess I'll go along with that.'

'You've seen him?' He detected a note of excitement in her voice.

'Yeah, I caught up with him after Suter got killed.' He glanced at her face, expecting to see a gleam in her eyes but she was looking at him gravely. 'Maybe I was wrong, but I persuaded him to head back to my place. If you want to see him you can ride out any time.'

'Aren't you taking a chance? If folk find out you're hiding him, then they're going to treat you as an accomplice.' Her remark surprised him but he shrugged his shoulders.

'Who's to tell? Grant and Rogers are pretty tight-mouthed and so long as Des keeps out of sight there's nothing to worry about.'

Sheila's hand rested lightly on his arm and as the feather-like touch sent a surge of excitement running through him he had trouble keeping the animation out of his face.

'You've always been a good friend, Jack.' He swallowed hard and the excitement drained away. Friend. Yes, that is what he had always been and that was his limit. 'But what if Des really did kill Jeff and the sheriff, are you still going to side him?'

'What would you want me to do?' The question came quickly and surprised himself as much as the girl. He felt her eyes probing him and grinned despite his feelings as he saw the look of dismay on her face.

'I – I don't know, Jack – I guess I'd have to leave you to do what you wanted.'

They stood in awkward silence for a minute or so then Sheila's hand touched his arm and she was gone. Mallory stared at the closed door briefly, then with mixed feelings headed back down the street.

When he untied his albino just below the Maverick a knot of men who had just emerged from the saloon stared down at him and he felt their resentment. He knew them all, had been friendly with them a long time but there was no mistaking their anger. They had it on good authority that Des Willard had killed Suter and they resented Mallory's categorical denial of the fact. He swung himself into the saddle and raised his hand before heading out of town, but nobody returned the salute.

As he rode along the south trail he considered things. Suter had been a popular lawman and Butane townsfolk would grow angrier still during the next few days. If he kept out of their way, maybe their rancour against him would fade, but if Des Willard showed himself then he, Mallory, could expect to get caught up in the blaze of feeling against his pard. The memory of Sheila Scott stayed with him too, his mind almost conjured up the sweet scent of her as his blood moved faster. The fleeting thought that he should throw Des Willard to the wolves he stifled with an exasperated oath as with an effort he dragged his mind back to tomorrow's meeting with the horse buyer, but although his solvency depended upon that event he could only give it partial consideration.

Shortly after taking the fork off the main trail he met Rogers, who was heading for town. They exchanged greetings as they pulled their mounts to a stop and Mallory regarded the older man carefully in the fading light.

'Better take care in town, Mike,' he said. 'The folk are right behind Manning, Dainton and the others who say Des Willard killed Suter. I guess I've riled them some by saying I didn't believe the evidence, so they might try to take it out on you.'

Mike Rogers grinned and shrugged his wide shoulders.

'Glad you told me, Jack,' he replied. 'Always

best to know what to expect. I guess this is one time when I'm not going to give an opinion one way or another. That way I reckon I should get myself a quiet drink and a couple of hands of cards.'

'I don't have to ask you to keep quiet about Willard being at the Triple Bar, but I guess you've got the right to give me your opinion about his guilt or innocence.'

Rogers did not answer at once and a frown of concentration creased his sunburned forehead.

'Nope. I can't figure Willard being a killer, except from an even start.' He looked up, his face serious. 'Anyways, if you believe in him enough to stick your neck out then it's good enough for me.'

'Maybe – but you don't have to take sides.' There was a warning in Mallory's voice but Rogers' glance was sharp when he replied.

'Now Suter I could go along with, but any side that's ranged against Manning and Dainton gets my support when the chips are down.'

Rogers kneed his mount into action and Mallory watched him ride towards town until a bend in the trail hid him from view. The man's solid support warmed the horse-rancher and he rode the rest of his journey in a happier frame of mind.

Mike Rogers found the atmosphere cool

when he entered the Maverick saloon. Men who normally exchanged cheerful greetings with him stared suspiciously out of cold eyes, and Con Sullivan, the barkeep, took his time moving up the bar to serve him. Sullivan's face held a silent warning as he passed a glass of rye across the counter. The hubbub of conversation that Rogers had heard when he had tied his mount to the hitchrail outside had faded the moment he pushed through the batwing doors, so he guessed the talk had been about his boss and Des Willard. He hunched his shoulders resignedly and gave his attention to the rye. Slowly the talk started up again and snatches of conversation drifted to him that gave his urbanity a jolt. Hard things were being said about Jack Mallory for not having helped Manning and Dainton by collecting cayuses for them, and also for not having brought Willard in. It seemed generally accepted that he had actually caught up with Willard, then allowed his pard to keep running.

'It's the same as backing Willard's play an' I reckon Mallory should be taught his lesson.' Ike Somers, the Lazy Q boss, made sure Rogers heard him as he leaned towards his cronies, Hank Kershawe and Dan Smeaton.

'Yep, he's gotta be taught he can't buck Butane folk without paying.' Hank Kershawe who owned the Stageline pitched in his piece

19

with obvious enjoyment. He seemed to thrive on making trouble.

Mike Rogers willed himself to stay with his drink but his taste for liquor was gone. Slowly he turned to stare at Somers and his two sidekicks. The Lazy Q man leered back at him evilly. Even before he spoke Rogers knew Somers' angle. The Lazy Q abutted on Triple Bar territory and the water Somers depended upon sprung from the hills on the Triple Bar. If Mallory could be moved on, then Somers would crowd in.

'You're sure talking a lot of hot air, Ike,' Rogers said easily. 'Just how do you aim to teach Jack Mallory anything? I reckon he's got the edge on you in any sort of show-down.'

'That's as maybe.' There was an evil glitter in Somers' eyes. 'But if folk feel the same way as me we'll run him outa the territory. Any man siding a hombre what's killed a lawman can expect to get moved on.'

'You talk like you're responsible for the conscience of Butane, Somers.' Mike growled. 'Well, Butane got along mighty fine before you showed up, which isn't so long ago. You just remember, Mallory is Butane born and bred and maybe when folk get to thinking straight, they won't be so keen to listen to your claptrap.'

A lot of men had stopped talking and crowded in to listen but, as Rogers glanced around them, he realised he would get no support for his boss.

'It looks like you're siding Willard too, Rogers.' This time it was Dan Smeaton who spoke up and his voice held a razor-edge quality. 'Maybe you think it was a good idea to plug Suter?'

'Suter was a friend of mine and well you know it,' Rogers snapped. 'I'd hold no brief for any man who killed him without giving an even chance, but until I heard a jury say Willard was guilty, then I'm ready to say he didn't do it.'

There was a howl of protest and Mike Rogers began to feel a trifle lonely. Dan Smeaton stood up and stepped close to Rogers. He was a husky, hard-looking man who made a living out of trading with the Kiowa Reservation Indians. He had seen plenty of trouble in his time but at thirty-six still had a taste for it.

'I guess we ought to start by running you outa town, Rogers,' he snarled. 'That way there'll be one gun less when we call on Mallory.'

Mike Rogers took a deep breath. He knew Smeaton to be a rare handful but he felt he was in with a chance once the chips were down.

'Why don't you quit talking about what the folk of Butane should do, just stick to what you'd like to do on your own account.'

The glint of battle showed in Rogers' eyes as he spoke. 'Maybe you'd like to try running me out of town on your lonesome.'

Smeaton made no reply but with the speed of a serpent's tongue his right hand flashed upwards, catching Rogers in the Adam's apple. Rogers staggered drunkenly against the bar and Smeaton got in close, thumping heavy blows to the body. With an effort, Mike Rogers resisted the impulse to let his mind take refuge behind the swimming mists threatening to engulf him and instinctively lunged vicious blows in the general direction of his attacker. A couple found a billet but Smeaton did no more than grunt, then come closer again, crowding and spoiling. The mists cleared and suddenly Rogers was fighting mad, his tongue ranged over his split lips, tasting the salt tang of blood and his sudden urgent desire was to batter Smeaton to a pulp.

His flurry of blows pushed Smeaton back and, as the man bounced forward again, he brought a ripping left hook up to the throat that had Smeaton glassy-eyed, as his right followed to the point of the chin, sending Smeaton sprawling over a table his head seemed to explode and, out to the world, he staggered a bit before slipping to the ground. Con Sullivan the barkeep leaned over the bar, still holding the bottle of rye that had spelt curtains for Rogers and eyed his victim without enthusiasm. Sullivan held Rogers in high esteem and he had reasoned, with the crowd in ugly mood, he would serve Rogers best by rendering him unconscious.

As half-hearted attempts were made to revive Dan Smeaton, Manning, Tyler and Creasey came through the doors and up to the bar. The crowd were shouting their intention to run Mallory out of town and the three newcomers exchanged satisfied glances. Manning held up his hand for silence and after a time the noise decreased sufficiently for him to make himself heard.

'The law can't prove Mallory helped Willard any so the law has no quarrel with him. Any opinions you hombres have are your own an' just see that if you get around to running him off the territory you don't hurt him any.' The lawman was playing himself a hand that could not lose. He was absolving himself from any responsibility for possible events whilst egging the crowd on to get rid of a possible source of danger to him and Dainton. He indicated the prostrate Rogers. 'I reckon he'll do best in the hoosegow for a day or so. He sure caused some ruckus.'

The crowd fell aside as Tyler and Manning grabbed hold of Rogers and carried him out of the saloon. Creasey took a gulp of bourbon and turned to Ike Somers and Hank Kershawe.

'I guess Manning's right,' he said loud enough for all to hear. 'We've got no call to hurt Mallory, but I reckon burning that hoss-ranch of his would persuade him he's not wanted in Butane any more than his murdering sidekick is.'

The idea took on and the crowd surged to the bar intent upon celebrating beforehand. Creasey slipped out after a time and reported to Manning at the gaol-house.

Sheila Scott looked up in surprise as her father came into the living-room a full hour earlier than usual. There was a disgruntled air about him as he struggled out of his black Albert and reached into the closet for his dressing-gown.

'You're early, Father,' the girl remarked. 'The meal's not nearly ready yet.' Ezra Scott poured himself a liberal measure of rye and took a draught before replying.

'Yeah. No pleasure being in the Maverick tonight. Lot of wild talk going on there, and folk who should know better are priming themselves up for a load of mischief.' Sheila felt her colour drain away as she realised the implications of her father's remarks. In view of recent events she was sure that any mischief would be directed towards someone she held in high regard.

'What mischief, Father?' her voice was flat.

'Running Jack Mallory out of the territory, they're talking now of burning his ranch down.'

'Oh, no!– What's Jack done?'

'Seems he helped Des Willard to keep running and folk don't take kindly to the way he talked to the men who saw Suter's killing. They took some spite out of Rogers and Manning's locked him up.'

Near panic sent a circle of thoughts pounding through the girl's mind. If the crowd rode out to Mallory's ranch they would find Des Willard there too, then there would be no stopping them. Both Mallory and Des Willard would be strung up without regard for the processes of the law. Only one course was open to her, she would have to warn them.

'I'm going to warn Jack Mallory, Father,' she blurted. 'Somebody's got to warn him so it might as well be me.'

Ezra Scott topped up his glass with rye and gazed at his daughter thoughtfully. Every instinct told him to refuse his permission but to his credit he recognised the urgency in the girl's mind. He spared a moment to mentally curse the injury sustained a few years earlier that debarred him from forking a cayuse, then the smile his daughter loved spread across his features.

'Go if you must, Sheila, but skirt the town and only join the trail if it's safe. Ride Dandy, he's black enough that he'll take some seeing and he's a mighty careful runner.' Sheila stepped forward impulsively and kissed him lightly on the cheek, then hurried to the door. Briefly she paused.

'I'll take care – don't worry.'

The door slammed behind her and Ezra Scott smiled in a wry fashion as he extracted a cigar from the cedar-wood box on the hand-carved sideboard. His only daughter taking her chance racing against time over fifteen miles of rough country without a glimmer of moonlight to ease the danger, and she tells him not to worry. No matter how much rye he might sink this night he knew he would worry until the moment his girl returned. When he heard her ride away he changed back out of the dressing-gown into his Albert again and left the house. Sheila needed time, so any delaying tactics he could employ in the Maverick would improve her chances.

Chapter Two

Sheila Scott had no trouble clearing the town without bumping into anyone. Judging by the noise coming from the saloons and particularly the Maverick, folk were still building up the sort of courage required to burn down the ranch-house of a man who had been around Butane since childhood, then to run him out of town. Her mount Dandy, her father's black gelding, was as sure-footed as a bighorn sheep and as the last light of Butane disappeared from view behind a clump of junipers, she eased the reins, giving the animal its head.

Although the sky was a blaze of light from stars that seemed to hang within reach, the light did not penetrate to ground level and the girl guided her mount by instinct and memory. She had ridden often enough to the Triple Bar and Box Q, so it was not surprising that she found her way unerringly to the trail within a mile of the fork to the Triple Bar. She was only yards away from the fork when Dandy almost came to a stop and pulled to the side of the trail. Sheila stared ahead and saw the deeper black of riders and horses against the dark blackcloth of night. She pulled Dandy to a halt just a few yards from the motionless riders ahead.

'Keep acoming,' a man's deep voice ordered. 'Let's get to know each other.'

The momentary panic Sheila felt subsided a little at the sound of the voice, she sensed a quality of goodness in the man. Pressing her knees into her mount's side she edged alongside the two riders.

'A lady eh. It sure must be peaceable here-abouts for a lady to be riding at night on her lonesome. Well, you've nothing to fear from us. That right, Sal?'

'Sure is right, Father.' Sheila's breath came in a gasp of relief at the sound of a woman's voice. 'I'm mighty relieved to know that,' she said quickly. 'I certainly was worried.'

'Tell me, ma'am, just how far is Butane? My reckoning makes it about seven miles.'

'Seven miles is near enough, but I wouldn't head that way right now if I were you.'

'And why not?' It was the girl who asked.

'Your father was just saying it's peaceable in this territory – well, I guess he couldn't be more wrong. In a short time from now just anybody who can ride a horse will be head-ing out of Butane to burn down a ranch-house and run the owner out of town. I'm hoping to get there ahead of them.'

The man grunted as though something vexed him. 'Had to see a hombre in Butane

28

tomorrow,' he said. Then out of consideration for the girl, he asked, 'Is it your family they're burning out?'

'No, just a friend.'

'Well, my name's Seth Dormer an' the young firebrand alongside me is my daughter, Sal. Suppose you tell us who you are and all about your problems.'

Despite Sheila's anxiety to get going she felt an irresistible urge to unburden herself and first diffidently, then more eloquently, she told Dormer and his daughter about the troubles besetting her friends Willard and Mallory. Neither father nor daughter interrupted her story, but as she finished, Dormer laughed a trifle bitterly.

'I guess that's the way it always happens,' he growled. 'Mallory is the man I was set to do business with tomorrow. We always seem to get caught up in some devilry or another no matter what town we hit.'

His daughter's musical laugh made Sheila stare in her direction, but it was too dark to make out her features. 'You know well enough, Father, you'd be disappointed if there were no complications to a trade.' There was a pause then. 'What do we do now?' she asked.

'Only one thing to do. We'll ride along with Miss Scott and lend Mallory a hand. We need those cayuses he's selling.'

As they turned their mounts and followed

29

when Sheila sent Dandy forward the girl felt the load lighten a little from her shoulders. Even though she could not see them, there was an aura of dependability about the horse-trader and his daughter that served to lift the chances for Willard and Mallory.

The daughter, Sal Dormer, was an excellent companion and rode alongside Sheila while her father dropped back a bit. She chatted in a gay, unaffected manner so adroitly that she kept Sheila's mind away from the main worrying problems right until they cleared the windbreak above the home paddocks and rode down into the compound formed by the ranch-house and outbuildings. Mallory was at the door as soon as the animals hit the iron-hard square, and as the riders dismounted below the verandah, he was standing at the top of the steps. The light from the doorway revealed Sheila Scott as she led the way to the steps, and Mallory grunted his surprise. He looked past her to the other two figures, then back to the girl as she stopped beside him.

'What in the heck are you doing here this time of night?' Mallory's voice was harsh. 'And who's with you?'

Dormer's tall figure loomed beside Sheila before she could reply, and Mallory could see the other arrival was a girl.

'The name's Dormer – Seth Dormer, an'

this is my daughter, Sal. I guess you must be Mallory?'

'Yeah – I'm Mallory.' The horse-rancher suddenly became aware of the courtesies and stood aside after shaking hands briefly with father and daughter. 'Come right on in.'

They all stepped inside the big living-room and were drawn irresistibly to the log-fire that filled the air with a pleasant resinous aroma. Sheila's eyes roved around the heavy furniture, noting the lack of decoration that a woman's hand would have altered, before fixing on Jack Mallory, who was studying Dormer with interest.

'Dormer, eh,' he mused. 'Then you're the horse-dealer I'm supposed to meet tomorrow?'

'Yeah, that's right. But I guess if I'd gone straight on to Butane without meeting up with Miss Scott my journey would have been wasted.' Mallory's glance was puzzled.

'How come wasted?'

Dormer shrugged and nodded towards Sheila.

'I'm afraid that's true, Jack,' she said hurriedly. 'There's been a lot of wild talk in town and they're coming here to burn you out, then run you out of the territory. Rogers got into a fight and Manning's put him in the jailhouse.'

Mallory's expression was incredulous for a few moments, then his face set in hard lines.

'Somebody's going to buy a lot of grief if they try that,' he remarked, then mindful of his duties he indicated the bottle of bourbon on the heavy sideboard. When Dormer smiled his pleasure Mallory filled a couple of glasses and handed one to the horse-dealer. 'Maybe you'd like to make a brew of coffee, Sheila, for yourself and Miss Dormer.'

'There's no time for coffee.' Sheila stamped impatiently. 'What are you going to do?'

'Sit tight, I guess, and throw plenty of lead when they show up,' Mallory grunted.

'That's what they want you to do I reckon,' Dormer put in. 'Miss Scott gave me the brief details and I'd say somebody's mighty anxious to get rid of you. Standing your ground against a townful of folk seems like playing into that somebody's hands.'

'Can't see that I've got much choice,' Mallory said flatly.

'Well, now, maybe I can give you a choice. My boys are camped about ten miles from here. If you've got those cayuses handy we could head 'em away right now and we'd be pleased to have you stay along until you've sorted out what action to take.' Dormer grinned and made himself a cigarette one-handed. 'If it was me, I'd head the cayuses just far enough out of harms way for now, then wait somewhere to see who was head-ing the hell-raisers. I guess the fire will show 'em up, then I'd do some riding an' set fire to their homesteads so you'd be all square come morning.'

'My God! You're right, Dormer!' There was a bitter smile on Mallory's face as he spoke.

'He always is right, Mr Mallory.' Sal Dormer spoke up in a calm, matter-of-fact manner, and Mallory looked at her for the first time. She had slipped the hood of her waterproof cloak off her head, revealing thick wavy hair of spun gold, and dark brown eyes gleaming with a lively intelligence, contrasting nicely with the pink skin and shapely red lips. She was worth looking at and Mallory coloured a little as he realised he had stared a mite too long. Sal Dormer did not appear to notice but Sheila Scott appraised the girl again and turned her glance to Mallory in an attempt to gauge the degree of his interest.

'I reckon I'll take a chance on you being right this time, Dormer,' Mallory said decisively. 'The broncs are corralled in a pasture alongside the river a couple of miles away, we could move 'em out pronto.' He paused and took another critical look at Dormer before continuing. 'If I move out, my pard comes with me, and right now he's wanted for a couple of killings.'

'Wanted is one thing, did he do the killings?'

Mallory shook his head decisively. 'He says not and I believe him.'

'I guess he's welcome to ride along, but I'll

make my own mind up whether he stays at camp or not.'

Dormer's face was bland when Mallory glanced at him but the eyes that looked back unblinkingly were grey, cool and dependable, and the horse-dealer's lined, craggy face simply oozed strength and character. Jack Mallory opined Dormer's reasons would be well based if he ultimately refused to let Des Willard stay. He pushed the bottle across the table towards Dormer and went through a doorway into another room. In the couple of minutes that elapsed before Mallory returned with Des Willard, Dormer fetched a couple more glasses and pouring out small measures handed them to the girls.

'Could be a busy night, a little drop might keep you on your toes.'

Sal Dormer took hers and downed it at a gulp without the slightest grimace but Sheila treated hers with more care. When Mallory came back into the room his eyebrows went up as he saw her with the glass to her lips. She caught his eye and a red flush stole up from her neck, then Willard followed through the doorway.

'My pard, Des Willard,' Mallory said simply. 'Seth Dormer and his daughter.'

Des shook hands first with Dormer whose appraisal was critical, then Sal Dormer's small hand was lost in his grip. Their eyes met briefly but they each in one moment

34

seemed to plumb the other's depths. As Willard turned to greet Sheila, Sal Dormer's eyes followed him. She liked the breadth of his shoulders, the sun-tanned handsome face and the crisp, curly blond hair that spilled over his forehead. Seth Dormer noticed her interest and had a moment's misgivings; he'd seen plenty of killers in his time and some had been good lookers.

'Get the broncs saddled up Des while I sort out what I want to take along.' Seeing Willard and Sheila close in animated conversation made Mallory's voice brusque. 'If we're going to get clear before the townsfolk show up we'd better get moving.'

'I guess you're right, Jack.' Des turned away from Sheila as he spoke and hurried outside while Jack crossed to the big bureau and rummaged through papers, selecting those things he wanted saved from the inevitable fire. Dormer continued to smoke and drink in a calm, detached way but the two girls found difficulty in regaining an easy manner with each other; they both felt that their interests would clash at some time in the future and the reserve started to build up in each of them.

As Willard appeared in the doorway Mallory thrust the last of the papers into a satchel. He took a swift look around the room, then with a shrug started for the door. 'I guess the next house'll be built more under

35

the shelter of that windbreak,' he growled and Sheila's heart ached with compassion for him. No matter how much he made light of things she knew the loss of his ranch-house would go hard with him.

A couple of minutes later they rode out of the compound and headed north. Mallory found himself up front with a girl on either side while Dormer and Des Willard rode together. The shyness Mallory felt with Sheila made him direct his conversation more to Sal Dormer and her replies were easy-going and unaffected so it appeared to Sheila that they were finding some pleasure in each other's company. The effect was to make her retire into her shell and she rode busy with her thoughts and hunched in the saddle against the cold.

Seth Dormer got down to cases quickly with Des Willard. Expertly he led the conversation along until he had the full picture clear in his mind. If Willard was speaking the truth then it looked as though the familiar pattern was emerging. Someone big pulling the strings and giving the orders ready to muscle in on somebody else's property. The intention to burn down Mallory's ranch-house probably emanated from the same source that had spelt trouble for Willard.

'This spread of yours, the Box Q, just how far away is it?' Dormer asked after a few minutes silence.

'Just a few more miles,' Des replied. 'The Triple Bar borders the Box Q. Why do you want to know?'

'Looks like we might have our camp on your territory,' Dormer said. It was no answer to Willard's question and the horse-dealer posed another. 'Would any of your hands back your play in a showdown?' Willard's laugh was hollow.

'I guess the last couple of straight-shooting top-hands left the Box Q about five years ago. They had stuck just as much of Jeff as they could stand. Their sympathy on account of the bullet wound in his skull when Ma and Pa got gunned in the stagecoach hold-up sure dried up at last, and they moved on. Since then we've made do with what we could get. It wouldn't surprise me if they've thrown a wide loop around the beef by now an' lit out for Sedalia.'

'Maybe we can move in and side you for a couple of weeks, I guess I'm ahead of schedule.' Des looked across at Dormer but the darkness hid the man's face and he turned away again thoughtfully. What was behind the horse-dealer's offer? Why should anyone shelve his business to shoulder a stranger's burden? What was his angle? These and a host of other questions flashed through his mind, yet overall the sure knowledge that he needed help bludgeoned his brain and the picture of Sal Dormer kept recurring. If he accepted the offer of help, then the girl would be mighty close at hand. He gave a wry grin, a fleeting acquaintance with Sal Dormer would be poor consolation when a noose was tightening on his neck.

'I'm sure obliged to you for offering your help, Mr Dormer, but there's no call for you to get caught up in my troubles.'

'Maybe not, but there've been times when I've leaned on other folk mighty heavily so I guess it's time I offered to do the shoring up.'

Willard smiled at Dormer's reply. It was disarming enough to get his agreement to the offer of help but he did not believe that Dormer had ever found the need to rely on anybody else. They relapsed into silence and a few minutes later rode alongside a big corral. Mallory pulled up beside the gate and a dark form dropped down to the ground from the top bar.

'Hiya, Hal. It's me – Mallory – with some company.'

'Howdye, Jack – I didn't expect you until the morning.'

Mallory introduced Hal Grant to the horse-dealer and his daughter and broke the news about the fire-raisers. Grant did not appear unduly perturbed.

'Well, the broncs are corralled right here, Dormer,' Mallory said. 'Shall we move 'em out?'

'Mebbe and mebbe not.' Dormer's voice sounded pensive.

'What do you mean?' Mallory was impatient.

'Well, I've been thinking. You and Willard are pards and your spreads run next to each other. It seems to me you might just as well amalgamate your interests. Move into the Box Q with Grant and Rogers, then you'll have all your guns in one place.'

'That's a wonderful idea, Mr Dormer,' Sheila Scott exclaimed excitedly. Then a dubious note came into her voice. 'But Des can't stay there, the sheriff will be constantly checking up on the Box Q.'

'You mean the deputy.' Willard's voice had an edge of bitterness. 'Don't forget I killed Suter.' The others let his remark pass but there was an awkward silence for a moment. 'I guess that seems like throwing your help back in your teeth,' he remarked in a more level manner. 'I'm sure sorry. It would suit me fine if we set up in the Box Q.'

'It's all right by me too, Des,' Mallory rejoined.

'In that case leave the broncs right where they are and I'll move camp,' Dormer put in. 'My men will herd these in close to your headquarters come daylight.'

'Suits me,' Mallory grunted. 'And I'll head back now to see the homestead go up.'

'Me too,' Willard said tersely.

'And me,' Hal Grant added.

The moon slid into view at that moment, shedding a pale light over the little group and giving form to the horses enclosed in the large corral. It picked up the ribbon of river that marked the northern boundary of the corral, and caused the stars to lose something of their brilliance.

'You can depend Sal and I will see Miss Scott comes to no harm,' Dormer said. 'Just don't tangle with the hombres no matter what they do. Pick your time for getting even.'

'Take care!' Sheila Scott's voice was anxious, and Mallory looked across to see her hand go on Des Willard's arm. Willard's horse was right alongside hers but Mallory did not get around to thinking of the movement as involuntary reaction, to him it was a manifestation of her love for his pardner. He swallowed hard and turned his mount around ready to move off. They waited while Grant saddled his horse, then with brusque farewells the group split up and rode off in opposite directions.

Mallory, Willard and Grant arrived at the juniper grove just above the Triple Bar no more than five minutes before the mob rode into the compound. They saw Ike Somers at the heart of the crowd, a lighted tallow torch in his hand. He yelled for Mallory to come out time and time again, then riding in close

40

he smashed a window with his gun-butt and threw the torch inside. Other blazing torches followed and flames started to engulf the building. Hubert Dainton showed up briefly in the shadows alongside another but unrecognisable rider.

As the mob exulted, the three men headed for Ike Somers' Lazy Q, and two hours later, their faces covered with bandannas, they surprised Ed Rollo the cook, Mathers, Lewin and Starr by bursting into the bunkhouse and rousting them into the compound with their belongings. Then while Mallory and Grant checked the ranch-house and released stabled animals Willard covered the crew with his .38s.

Starr, who always kept a derringer inside his shirt could not resist making a play for it and got a smashed shoulder for his pains from the watchful Willard. His screams of anguish were drowned by the amazed shouts of his confederates as the flames started to lick up the buildings. Somers' men watched in disbelief as Mallory threw a spirit lamp into the bunkhouse, and shouted puerile threats while the marauders left them minus their gunbelts.

Chapter Three

It needed about an hour to sun-up when Willard, Mallory and Hal Grant dismounted on the edge of the compound opposite the Box Q ranch-house. Normally at this time there would have been some movement, but no one and nothing stirred. They left their mounts ground-hitched and crossing the compound entered the ranch-house quietly. When the door opened they were met with a blast of stale, liquor-laden air and the snuffles and snores of sleeping men told them the Box Q hands were taking things easy.

'Better get yourself out of sight, Des,' Mallory whispered. 'We'll get this lot sorted out.'

Willard made no reply but in the pale light that filtered through the windows Mallory saw him move cautiously around the room then push the door open to the place his brother Jeff had used for an office. With the door shut, Jack Mallory reached for a lamp and, lighting it, placed it on the table. He and Hal Grant stared around the room in disgust. Half a dozen men lay in drunken sleep on the Navajo rugs with empty bottles strewn around them. Cigarette butts littered the floor and playing-cards were spread across the table.

When Mallory lit two more lamps that were suspended from the thick cross-beams, a couple of the sleeping men stirred and stared up owlishly. Sam Genner, Jeff Willard's segundo, eyed Mallory uncomprehendingly for a full minute, then the mists seemed to clear and he staggered to his feet. His movements were a bit premature after his drinking spree and he had to clutch at the table to keep his balance.

'Well – what in tarnation do you want?' he growled.

'I want you to kick the rest of this crummy outfit onto their feet and set them about the job they were hired for,' Mallory replied brusquely.

Genner bristled and he threw off the effects of the liquor with the cowboy's unrivalled facility. 'And what makes you think I'll take your say-so?' he asked. The other men were awake now and one after another hauled themselves erect.

'If you pack anything faster than these, Genner, you don't have to take my say-so.' Mallory tapped his guns meaningly. 'And that goes for any other hombre.' Genner looked hard at Mallory but his eyes wavered a bit, the Triple Bar man had been known to take the pips out of the three of spades before most folk could clear leather. 'Des Willard's my pard and I don't aim to see his spread go to ruin while he's clearing himself with the law.' Mallory's voice was cold. 'And until he comes back I'm gonna run this outfit.' He paused to let the fact sink in, then continued. 'So like I said before, get moving and get busy.'

Genner shrugged his shoulders, then nodded to his men and indicated the door. The others grouped behind him. They stopped at the doorway and turned as Mallory spoke again.

'Another thing, Genner, if you or any other man step inside this ranch-house again without being asked you'll get a bellyful of lead. Stick to the bunkhouse.' The segundo pushed his way through the little knot of men, and now his face was hard.

'You're sure carving yourself out a handful of trouble, Jack Mallory. There's nothing you can do to stop us quitting the Box Q so I reckon you an' Grant can start running it on your lonesomes.'

'That suits me fine, Genner. You've just quit, so get your warbags packed and hit the trail.'

Genner stood a long time staring at the horse-rancher, but Mallory was unruffled. The man opened his mouth to say something, then thought better of it and turning abruptly, bundled the other men outside.

Hal Grant followed after them on to the verandah to keep track of their movements, and Des Willard joined Mallory from the inner room.

'If Genner's gonna stay in this territory you'll have to keep your eyes skinned for him. He'll put a bullet in your back at the first chance.' Mallory shrugged and reached for his tobacco sack.

'Not Genner– He's loud-mouthed, he'd have to get the drop on a hombre an' use up a lot of time talking about what he's going to do.' Des Willard's face expressed some doubt as he searched a cupboard for a bottle.

'Don't place too much reliance on that,' he grunted, then after bringing a bottle of rye to the table and eyeing the state of the table and the surrounding rug. 'I guess this place needs a clean-up before I could stomach a drink, let's go into the kitchen.'

After opening the door to the kitchen they were about to enter it when Mallory held Willard's arm and pointed to the deep leather chair in the corner. Squinty Robins, the cook, was in the depths of a drunken sleep. A couple of empty bottles lay at his feet and another bottle half-full stood on the end of the big black cooking range within reaching distance. Mallory edged Willard back into the living-room, then letting the door shut, lit a lamp.

Easing out one of his guns he placed the cold muzzle against Squinty's temple, then he gave the cook a sharp kick on the shin.

Squinty snuffled a couple of times then came to life. His eyelids opened and awareness showed immediately in his eyes. There was nothing wrong with his reflexes, the nerve messages to his brain from the area covered by the cold ring of steel gave him the picture so that even though his glance swivelled to find Mallory he did not move a muscle.

'The party's over, Squinty,' Mallory rasped. 'You just get on to your dawgs an' clean this place up.'

'An' who says you can give the orders?' Squinty could be mean at a pinch. Mallory pressed the gun muzzle a little deeper. 'This says so, Squinty, and in case you're thinking I wouldn't kill anyone in cold blood you might as well know things have changed a mite lately an' I guess I've changed too.' Squinty was trying hard to focus both eyes on Mallory. 'Tonight, Butane folk burned out the Triple Bar so I've run clear out of sympathy for anyone. If you want to stay healthy just clean this place up like I said then get a meal going.'

'An' who pays me?' Squinty's tone was conciliatory.

'I do. Now if that answers all your questions, get busy.' Mallory holstered the gun as he spoke and Squinty came to his feet. The cook reached for the half-full bottle and took a couple of hefty swallows then squared his shoulders.

'Righto, Mallory. I guess it don't matter two cusses who I work for so long as my pay's on the line.'

Jack Mallory was not fooled any, he knew just how close Squinty Robins was with Dainton and Nolan but he reckoned some chances would have to be taken.

'Des Willard's here,' he remarked casually. 'And you're the only hombre except a couple of his pards who knows. If anyone comes here looking for him I reckon it'll be on account you've opened your mouth, so the first thing I'll do is ventilate you some.' Squinty's affliction became even more marked as he considered Mallory.

'It's nothing to me, Mallory,' he replied. 'And I guess if anyone comes alooking it'll be on account it's kinda natural for a man to head back for home. Most lawmen make regular calls on home territory for wanted men.'

This was true enough and Mallory knew it but he made no attempt to minimise his threat.

'After you get this place cleaned up the other room needs some tidying, Genner an' his sidekicks left in a hurry an' they sure left some mess.'

As he spoke they heard the clatter of horses' hooves as men rode away from the compound and Squinty's expression was aggrieved, it was pretty evident he would

47

have liked to be riding out with the others. Mallory ignored him and returned to the big living-room. Hal Grant came in off the verandah at the same time. Des Willard had cleaned the table down, so they gathered around it and took up the glasses that Des had filled.

'There were three more hombres in the bunkhouse,' Hal Grant said. 'But the whole outfit have ridden out.'

'I've got my doubts about any of your hands being on night trick, Des,' Mallory said after slaking his thirst. 'It looks like we'll have our hands full taking care of things.'

'Maybe there'll be no critturs left to wet nurse,' Des remarked. 'My bet is that Genner an' the rest will throw a loop around the main herd and head for Sedalia.'

Squinty Robins, who was listening at the door of the kitchen, looked murderous. If what Willard said was true then he was losing a fat share of dinero. He looked to the kitchen window and debated whether to make his departure by that route and burn leather to catch up with Genner. The next piece of conversation helped him make up his mind.

'In that case, Des, we've got to move pretty fast and get you cleared of the killings,' Mallory said.

'And how do you propose to do that?' Des asked.

'I guess Seth Dormer and his men would side us if we all rode into town and demanded that Suter's body be dug up and the slug taken out of his hide. If that slug is anything but a .38, then somebody else must have killed him.'

'Yeah!' It was obvious that Des Willard had not given thought to this before by the inflection in his voice. 'Why in heck didn't I think of that, Jack?'

Squinty's eyes narrowed. It was news to him that Suter was dead, but the implications were clear enough. Des Willard must have been alleged responsible for his death, and the fact that Des, like his brother Jeff, had always packed Adams .38 was well known. They got their ammunition direct by stage from the agents at Austin. Every other man in Butane packed Colt .45s. Squinty craned his neck to catch the rest of the conversation.

'It was clear enough to me that Dainton, Manning or one of the others must have done the killing if two shots had been fired at Suter,' Des continued after a pause. 'But I sure didn't think it would be easy to prove they're in cahoots.'

Robins moved away from the door and got down to the job of cleaning up the kitchen, the gleam of avarice was alight in his misaligned eyes and his desire to catch up with Genner was gone. He had just been handed a trump card that would pay him plenty with minimum effort. Just one chore to be done, one that would take some gall, after that, easy street. Then a nagging doubt assailed him as the first thin light of dawn made itself apparent. His chances of easy money depended upon darkness. If Willard and Mallory were to ride into Butane today then the chance was gone.

It was when he took in the hastily prepared breakfast that his mind was set at rest and Squinty became amiable enough to be taken as well disposed towards young Willard.

'Reckon you'd better get prepared for about twenty hungry horse-trailers,' Des said to him as Squinty slammed the coffee-pot down onto the table. 'They should be arriving in a couple of hours and I guess they'll want a good meal before hitting the hay.'

Squinty nodded and returned to the kitchen. These men must be the ones Mallory had said would side them in Butane, so if they needed shut-eye first, it was going to be nightfall before they would head for town. He gave a little laugh, he'd just have to work fast, that's all.

Amos Cotton, Dormer's scout, stood just below the rim of a dry-wash and waved Dormer forward. The two girls rode alongside the horse-dealer, then way behind them, nearly 500 head of horses moved along sweetly in the care of about twenty herders. With a word to the girls, Dormer rode on up the wash and dismounted alongside Cotton.

'Take a look, Seth,' Cotton said. 'Looks like a trail herd heading this way.'

Dormer peered over the rim to the vast spread of undulating terrain beyond, and, sure enough, the dust-cloud that spilled up just short of the haze that ended the range of vision, indicated a fair-sized herd on the move.

'Could be Willard's hands moving out and set on getting a big pay-day in Sedalia,' Dormer remarked. Cotton nodded. Dormer had explained the set-up to his men and they were all quite happy to take chips in the game. 'Ride back, Amos, and tell Cartmell to call a halt and bring half the lads back with you. I guess we'll check on this herd.'

Cotton grinned his delight and headed back to the steadily advancing lines of horses, pausing just long enough beside Sal Dormer and Sheila Scott to tell them to follow, then burned leather in his eagerness. The girls turned their mounts and rode more slowly.

Fifteen minutes later, a dozen men watched the herd now no more than a mile or so away from the rim of the wash. Dust spewed up and hung in a blanket over the herd but the leaders were plainly visible now, a couple of riders showed up on either flank but Dormer waited until the leaders were about 300 yards away, then he stood up and signalled his men to move. They were in their saddles and riding out of the wash in seconds. Amos Cotton and four men rode on ahead, waving their wide sombreros and yelling, making the lead steers falter then swerve. There were loud, dismal cries of protest from the depths of the herd as the leading cattle were turned in a tight circle back into the following cows. Then, encouraged by the rest of Dormer's men, the herd milled patiently.

With the cows under control, Dormer, Cotton and a couple of hands waited calmly for the riders who emerged out of the dust pall and rode furiously towards them. The riders hauled their mounts to a slithering stop just a few yards away and Dormer saw a few more men part company from the herd.

'What in heck do you hombres think you're doing?' Genner's eyes gleamed wickedly out of his dust-covered face as he addressed the question with unerring instinct at Dormer the leader.

'Stopping the drive so that we can ask a few questions.' Dormer replied imperturbably.

'Like what?' Genner fairly bristled.

'Like whose herd is this? And who's doing the droving? And where are you heading?'

There was a long minute when Genner just stared and the rest of his men pulled up behind him. More of Dormer's men had detached themselves from the herd and were heading for the opposing groups.

'It's Box Q beef.' Genner snapped. 'And I'm the Box Q ramrod, name's Genner, Sam Genner! An' I'm heading 'em for Sedalia.'

'You can head for Sedalia, Genner, you an' your sidekicks, but the beef stays on Box Q territory.'

'Listen, mister! You've got no call to stop this herd moving out, so just get your men aside so's we can get 'em moving again.' Genner spoke as though he was ready to let things pass as a joke, but no one was laughing and his face grew hard, he turned to his men and barked his orders. 'Get 'em started again.'

'Any man that moves dies!' Dormer's voice was laden with menace and the Box Q men froze in their saddles. 'That herd belongs to Des Willard and he's not available to give his say-so about heading his beef to Sedalia. That means just one thing in my book, you hombres are plain no-good rustlers.'

Genner looked startled. This man sure enough knew all the answers. He looked around the ring of faces, weighing up the chances of success if he should make a fight of it but the hard, uncompromising expression did nothing for his confidence. The iron went out of his manner and he shrugged his shoulders expressively. 'I guess you're entitled to think what you like,' he growled. 'But the last order Jeff Willard gave me before he got killed by his brother was to run a herd to Sedalia. If you want to head 'em back, then it's up to you.'

'It's up to me right enough, Genner,' Dormer said quietly. 'But just for interest sake, if you'd made Sedalia who would have had the dinero – Des Willard?'

'Sure.' Genner tried to make it sound genuine but the fury mounted in his face again when the men ringing Dormer laughed their disbelief. Dormer nodded mockingly.

'Well, we've saved you the chore, so you fellers can ride where you want, so long as it is off Box Q territory.'

Genner flashed a last look around his men but there was no enthusiasm for battle evident upon their faces, then with a resigned sort of look he kneed his mount forward. Dormer's men pulled their mounts aside to let him and his men through, then they followed on behind in a phalanx to see the rustlers on their way.

A couple of hours later, Dormer and his men rode into the Box Q compound. The herd grazed on the home range and the horses rested temporarily in the big corrals. Mallory, Willard and Grant came into the compound to greet them, then gave a hand to stable the saddle-horses while Sal Dormer and Sheila Scott went inside the house.

As the men groomed the trail dust out of their mounts, Dormer paused and eyed Willard, who was attending to Sheila Scott's black. 'We met up with your ramrod Genner an' the rest of your hands – they were herding a pretty big drive of your beef. I asked him where he was heading an' he said Sedalia.'

Des Willard's eyes were fever bright with the burning sense of frustration that flooded him but he said nothing. What could he do? Suddenly he felt he had made a mistake in coming back and it was some time before Dormer's next words sunk in.

'I reckoned that herd was on the hoof without your say-so an' I persuaded Genner to keep going without 'em. They're eating into the long grass that young Sheila says is your home graze. If you want, we'll spread 'em out a bit tomorrow.'

'I – I'm obliged, Dormer,' Des said after a long pause. 'You sure have the right ideas.' Dormer shrugged and gave his slow smile before getting back to the chore in hand.

When they crossed to the house, Dormer's men were ranged around a field-kitchen and chuck-wagon. They were all in high good humour and the pards and Grant were impressed with the solidarity that showed beneath the easy, good-natured chaffing being bandied around. Dormer had a pretty tight outfit.

Squinty Robins had cleaned up the big living-room and had a meal all ready for them when they entered the house. He kept the meal simmering while Willard poured out drinks to spin out the time until the two girls cleaned the trail dust out of their skin and clothes, and all the time Squinty kept his ears open. He heard what he wanted quickly enough.

'You've been good enough to offer your help, Dormer,' Mallory said after taking a drink. 'Well, if you'll side us we'll go into Butane and get Des off this Suter killing charge.' Dormer took a long drink before replying.

'I'll side you sure enough, but how do you aim to prove Willard didn't kill Suter?'

Des slid his guns out of his holsters and handed them to the horse-dealer. 'There's the proof, Dormer. The only Adams .38s packed in Butane belong to me, Jeff used 'em too. We get our shells brought in from Austin, the last case we had is in that chest.' Des nodded to a large redwood chest that had a leather seat fastened to its lid. 'If I killed Suter, then he's got a .38 slug in his chest. Jack says we should ride in and get Doc Colehan to dig that slug out of his body; that way we can prove the killing was done by the men who rode with him.'

'It's sure worth the try,' Dormer replied. 'My men'll need some shuteye and I reckon the same goes for you. Me and Amos Cotton will head into town with young Sal and Miss Sheila after we've eaten. Miss Sheila's plumb concerned about her pa, who'll be worried on her account and she's persuaded young Sal to stay at her place. If you'll bring in half of my outfit to arrive a couple of hours after sundown, Amos and me will be waiting for you. I guess the place to make for is the jailhouse. The rest of my outfit will look after things here.'

'We're sure obliged to you, Mr Dormer,' Des said earnestly. 'Maybe we'll get a chance to even the score some day.'

'Like I said before, I've had help many times, the only way to repay is to lend a hand yourself when you see the need, that way things kinda even out.'

At that moment the two girls came into the room and Dormer smiled inwardly as Mallory and Willard stared in admiration. The girls had removed all traces of dust and fairly glowed with good health. Sheila's dark beauty contrasted wonderfully with Sal's fair, elfin-like loveliness making an overall picture that made the younger men forget all about their troubles. Mallory's eyes met Sheila's, but, as usual, his shyness made him look away and she turned to make a comment to Des, who placed a chair for her. Dormer arranged the chair for Sal, who brought her glance back from contemplation of Des in a cool, easy manner that gave no indication of what she was thinking, then Des took his place between the two girls while Mallory sat opposite, next to Hal Grant.

Squinty Robins was a good cook at any time, but in an effort to lull Mallory and Willard into the belief he was content to stay put, he excelled himself and served up the meal in as cheerful a manner as he had ever managed before. Long before they had settled down to coffee and smokes, Mallory was congratulating himself that he had not slung Robins out along with Genner. Later when Dormer, Amos Cotton and the two girls rode out of the compound, Squinty sat in the shade on the verandah, dozing in apparent contentment.

Chapter Four

'There's sure some ruckus going on Seth,' Amos Cotton growled when they took the last turn in the trail that ran for the last quarter of a mile, as straight as a die, down the grade to the northern end of Butane.

There was no need for Dormer or the girls to comment; they all saw the crowd massed halfway down Main Street, and even at a quarter of a mile it was possible to gauge the mood by the wildly gesticulating men in the middle of the crowd.

'That's the jailhouse, I guess.' Sheila remarked. 'I hope they're not planning to do anything drastic to Mike Rogers. They're mean enough for anything now.'

Dormer made no reply, he had no intention of wasting his mental energies on conjecture; they would soon know what kept the folk of Butane grouped under the scalding heat of the sun at a time when they normally sought shade and solitude.

Nobody moved aside when the four riders nudged the edge of the crowd, so they drew rein and listened.

'I'll tell you, Willard was with Mallory!' The speaker's eyes fairly glittered as he shouted to the crowd. He stood on the sidewalk in front of the jailhouse, and close beside him was a man wearing a star on his vest. 'Rollo, Lewin and Mathers all swear the hombres were Willard and Mallory, ain't that no so? I guess we all know 'em well enough that covering their faces over wouldn't fool us any.'

'That's Ike Somers the Lazy Q man,' Sheila whispered to Dormer, as the three men close behind Somers nodded in confirmation.

'The bustards burned down all my buildings an' I aim to get square. The Box Q goes up in smoke tonight an' I'm taking enough Box Q beef to pay for a new set of buildings,' Somers ranted and glared around the crowd, waiting for yells of agreement but the crowd went suddenly quiet as Hubert Dainton edged alongside the Lazy Q man.

'Now you just take it easy, Ike,' Dainton said loudly. 'When Des gets what's coming to him the Box Q becomes mine. So just steer clear of the territory and keep your hands off Box Q critturs.'

Ike Somers stared at Dainton aghast, then his eyes narrowed. His plans to spread over Jack Mallory's horse-ranch would not meet with much success if Hubert Dainton took over the Box Q. Dainton was a dab hand at infiltration himself and every man on his payroll was eager enough to call the tune. Only Suter had prevented Dainton from becoming too ambitious since he started up the Diamond Flash brand with Martha Willard's money.

'Until Willard's caught, the Box Q is his,' Somers mouthed. 'And I aim to take what I reckon to be my due.'

Dainton shrugged his shoulders. 'You're gonna buy yourself a lot of grief, Ike,' he said smoothly. 'Ain't that so, Slim?' He turned to the lawman beside him, who nodded.

'Yeah, that's so. If you say Mallory and Willard burned your place down, then let's get 'em brought in and we can take it out of their hides before stretching their necks. That is after a jury's convicted 'em.'

Somers tried to bottle his fury, then it broke out anew as he turned his spite back to the architects of his misfortune. 'Let's start right in on Rogers,' he shouted. 'He knew well enough that Mallory was hiding Willard. He's in it plumb up to the neck. What say we string him up?'

Dainton and Manning kept quiet and a ripple of excitement ran through the crowd. Suter had kept folk in Butane on a tight rein for a long time and now, suddenly, the thought of some unrestricted violence met with an eager response from the savage depths of their natures. There were a number of men who knew and liked Mike Rogers but some of them found themselves carried along with the mood of the crowd and they shouted as loud as the rest to bring Rogers out.

61

Slim Manning held his hand aloft in a half-hearted attempt to gain the attention of the crowd but the words he uttered in paying mere lip-service to the law and the proper course of justice were lost in the roar as men surged forward to the jailhouse. The couple of shots Dormer loosed into the air had much better effect. The forward movement stopped and everyone turned to stare at the newcomers.

Upon Dormer's instructions Sheila and Sal had backed their horses well clear and Seth Dormer and Amos Cotton sat their mounts straight-backed and forbidding, their six-guns covered Somers, Dainton and Manning.

'The first man that moves a muscle dies!' Dormer's voice cut through the silence in a tone that spelt sudden death. 'You the lawman of this burg, mister?' Dormer's eyes rested briefly on Manning but he did not wait for a reply. 'I'm a Deputy US Marshal, Mister Lawman, and if these hombres make a move to get your prisoner I'll put a slug right through your middle. It's your job to see a prisoner gets a fair hearing.'

'I don't need you to tell me my job.' Manning just fell short of sounding convincing. There was something about Dormer that told him the man would back every word with action.

'Just tell 'em all to drift. Get the place emptied and you stay whole.' Dormer sounded contemptuous.

There was a flash of movement beside Manning as someone went for a gun, then a form lurched against Manning's shoulder and pitched to the sidewalk boards as both Dormer and Cotton fired simultaneously, a gun dropped from the fallen man's nerveless fingers to the street.

'Anybody else tired of living?' As Dormer asked the question the growl of protest at Lewin's death died away in every man's throat, and suddenly the urge to string Rogers up palled. A few men on the far edge of the crowd turned away slowly and moved off down the street, their hands noticeably well away from their sidearms. The idea caught on and in a remarkably short space of time only the men on the sidewalk remained, staring into the muzzles of the guns Dormer and Cotton held so menacingly. 'The rest of you hombres had better get the corpse to the funeral parlour.' Dormer said icily. 'My business is with the badge toter.'

'You going to let him push you around, Slim?' Ike Somers fairly screamed.

'Why don't you keep your big mouth shut, Ike?' It was Hubert Dainton who spoke. 'Lend a hand to tote Lewin away, I guess he had about as much sense as his blamed boss.'

Somers looked for one outraged moment

into Hubert Dainton's face and his blood ran cold. Dainton's face was a bland mask but the evil intent in his eyes left Somers no room for doubt. He tried to grin the remark away but it was a lop-sided, bitter effort and without further ado he growled instructions to Rollo to help him and Dainton pick up Lewin's body.

Dormer watched the little group head away for the funeral parlour, then he dismounted and tethered his mount to the hitchrail. 'See the girls home, Amos,' he said, then to Manning. 'You and me had better go inside the jailhouse.'

Manning's face was bleak but he said nothing and pushed the door open for Dormer to pass through. Seth Dormer shook his head and motioned with his gun for the Deputy Sheriff to precede him, so Manning stepped inside. Dormer followed him close, then bolted the door behind them. Manning sat down heavily and pulled a bottle of rye towards him; ostentatiously he poured one glass and drained it while Dormer took a seat opposite.

'This Rogers– What are you holding him for?'

'Creating a disturbance. He caused one heck of a ruckus in the Maverick saloon last night.'

'Anybody prefer charges?' Dormer's voice was smooth, lulling Manning temporarily, and he shook his head.

'Then you've got no call to hold him. He should have been tried this morning and either fined or not, then set free.'

'He's waiting to see the judge, mister, and he's not going to be back for a few days. And anyways who in heck are you?'

Seth Dormer extracted a badge from his vest pocket and tossed it on the table. 'Like I said I'm a US Deputy Marshal, and the name's Dormer – Seth Dormer. Now I'm telling you, unless Rogers caused injury to anyone or someone's preferring charges, you've got no call to keep him locked up. I didn't get your monicker.'

'It's Manning!' The deputy snarled the words. 'Just look here, Dormer, I run the law here now and I'll do things the way I see fit.'

A gleam came into Dormer's eyes that had a steadying effect on Manning's rising temper. 'Doing things your way, Manning, would have ended in a neck-tie party for a hombre who only caused a ruckus if I hadn't happened along. Well, just haul those keys down and turn Rogers loose.'

It was a full minute before Manning moved, a minute pregnant with hate and menace. A dozen times the Butane man called on his reserves of gall to refuse and each time he found himself wanting. There was something in Dormer's mocking face that robbed him of confidence. Then slowly he dragged himself to his feet and, taking a bunch of keys from a hook on the wall, he unlocked the dividing door between the office and cell block. Leaving the door ajar he unlocked a cell door, then stood aside. 'You can go, Rogers,' he snarled, 'And if you've got sense you'll head into the sun an' keep riding.'

Mike Rogers' bulk blotted Manning from Dormer's view as the released prisoner paused in the corridor, but Dormer had no difficulty guessing at Manning's expression as Rogers replied.

'It'd take a whole lot more than you, Manning to make me light out of town and I guess it'll take more than you to get me inside this calaboose again. I never did rate you very high an' the way you're taking sides I reckon you're a whole lot worse than I thought.'

'You can shoot off your mouth all you want, Rogers,' Manning answered shortly. 'But I brought you in here to save you from the townsfolk. They were all set to take it out on you for the way Mallory sided Willard.'

'Yeah!' Rogers snorted derisively. 'Like you'd have saved me from a lynching now, this pesky jailhouse isn't that thick a man can't hear what goes on outside.' Mike Rogers turned his back on Manning and entering the office section, hauled his gunbelt from off the nail that held it, then nodded affably at Dormer as he buckled it in place. 'I heard enough to know I'm obliged to you, mister,' he said. Then he tapped his guns. 'I guess I'll find out if any hombre still likes the idea of lynching Mike Rogers; it could be they've changed their minds for keeps.'

'I'll come along with you,' Dormer said with a smile, and ignoring Manning, who eyed them balefully, the two men moved out on to the sidewalk.

The street was deserted, apart from the line of horses that drooped under the sun's heat along the length of hitchrail, and a prairie schooner already loaded but waiting for the team of horses that were being shod at the Smithy. A couple of lizards scuttled out of the sun back into the shadow of the sidewalk as the two men walked along the street to the Maverick saloon. The heat was too great for much energy to be expended in shouting, so the muted sounds coming from the saloon was no guide to the size of the crowd inside, only the curling pall of cigarette smoke that drifted over the batwing doors gave the clue.

When Rogers pushed the doors aside and glared inside, it seemed that all of Butane was crowded into that one saloon. It took a full minute for his presence to be transmitted to the last man in the saloon but at the end of that minute he had everyone's attention. There were a few men shamefaced enough to shuffle. Dormer slipped into the saloon behind Rogers, then took a stand alongside him.

'Any of you hombres still wanting to lynch me?' Rogers' voice boomed around the saloon, his normally good-natured face was contorted into a mask of hate and his eyes were bright pinpoints of fire.

Nobody moved and nobody spoke. Rogers was not considered any great shakes with a gun but no one felt a test of skill was worth the risk. He had no recourse but to direct his attention to the group ranged at the centre of the bar.

'How about you, Dainton, an' you, Somers? I could hear you shouting for my neck, you still want to try something?'

'There's a whole lot of difference between talk an' doing, Rogers.' Hubert Dainton spoke evenly. 'You've got a whole skin and you ain't been hurt, nobody's tried to lynch you, so why don't you fork your freight outa town?'

'I'll do that when I'm good and ready, Dainton,' Rogers snarled. 'You haven't got much to say, Somers,' he went on. 'Seems you've dried up some after shouting so loud outside the jailhouse.'

Ike Somers' face was a study in indecision. The bully inside him fairly screamed to take

Rogers up because the outcome was a stone-walled certainty, he knew his speed with a six-gun was way ahead of Rogers, but somehow he felt that advantage was to be gained by evading the issue. Dainton had set the pattern and who was better at adding up the score than Dainton. The Lazy Q man conjured up a benign expression. 'Maybe I've done some thinking,' he answered. 'Maybe I was too quick to pass on the fault of Mallory's doings to his hands, but, like Dainton says, you ain't been hurt any.'

Rogers swallowed his rage slowly, short of going for his guns, there seemed no way to even up the score. He was searching for provocation when his companion came closer.

'I reckon a drink'll take away the taste of that jailhouse outa your system,' Dormer said. 'I guess you'll have to be content having 'em admit they were a mite hasty; nobody's gonna take you up on anything with me around.' He spoke quietly and Rogers' big frame relaxed.

The crowd fell away to allow the two men to get to the bar and, after a few minutes' awkward silence, the hum of conversation started up again. When Dormer and Rogers left a half an hour later everybody was busy talking and it seemed nobody noticed their going.

As the two men made their way to Ezra Scott's place, Dormer filled in the details of what had happened since Rogers had landed in the jail. The Triple Bar man's eyes glittered bitterly at hearing of the destruction of the ranch-house. 'The way things are hotting up in this territory it looks like there's gonna be a lot of powder burned mighty soon.'

'You could be right, Rogers,' Dormer agreed.

Ike Somers edged away from Hubert Dainton after Dormer and Rogers left the Maverick and contented himself with some hard drinking with Rollo and Mathews. Ed Slade, the teller at Ezra Scott's bank, took Somers' place beside Dainton and after ordering his usual brand of bourbon, eyed the crowd with his mild gaze.

'Finished for the day, Ed?' Dainton asked casually. Slade nodded.

'Yeah, it looked like business was finished anyway.'

The crowd was beginning to thin out as men went about their business and Slade made his way to a table. Dainton followed with the bottle. They drank in silence for about ten minutes, each apparently busy with his own thoughts.

'Manning tried to put the pressure on yet?' Slade asked at length. Hubert Dainton's smile was mean when he shook his head.

'He's going to be disappointed when he

does. He'll get his usual handout but that's as far as it goes. Anyway, he's smart enough to know he's in no position to put on the pressure. The moment he agreed to go along with eliminating Suter he was in the middle of it right up to the neck.'

'You're sure learning, Hubert,' Slade murmured, his face as benign as though he were talking small talk with a school-marm. 'Just let him know where he stands, but I guess the way things are moving it'll be dinero well spent to keep him eager to get elected sheriff. If he gets to thinking he'd like to ride to some place where it's healthier we might get another Suter on our necks.'

'Looks like we've got one,' Dainton replied slowly.

'You mean that Dormer hombre who sprung Rogers?'

'Yeah, he could be a lot of trouble to us,' Dainton replied thoughtfully. 'He sure enough had the crowd eatin' crow fast, I played along with him, I guess, but that was just good sense.'

'Dormer's main concern is horse-buying for the army,' Slade remarked. He took a long drink of bourbon before continuing. 'He's a US Deputy Marshal in a sort of spare time capacity, he's got a kind of roving commission to clean up the West. The way I heard it he's a close friend of Captain McCoy of the Rangers, but his business here was to buy

71

about sixty head of horses from Mallory.'

'So– It looks like he's taking sides.' A slow smile appeared on Dainton's face. 'Maybe I should pass on the information to Ike Somers that Mallory and Dormer are business acquaintances, Ike'll mebbe go off half-cock. That way, no matter who eliminates who, it'll help us some.'

'You've got a nice grasp of things, Hubert,' Ed Slade said silkily. 'Ike's spread isn't much but I reckon we could use it.'

Dainton made no reply and after filling his glass got up and crossed the room to where Somers was drinking himself silly. The Lazy Q man stared at Dainton suspiciously, but Dainton merely looked expansive. 'Looks like we got taken in, Ike,' he remarked. Then when Somers said nothing, he continued, 'That hombre Dormer is a horse-dealer and he's in Butane to buy up a bunch of Mallory's cayuses, it looks like he knew the score before he hit town.'

'How come you know this?' Somers' hot eyes searched Dainton's face.

'Slade says so. Seems there was a cash arrangement with the bank if Dormer took a shine to what Mallory was offering.'

'So his big law talk was plain moonshine, he sprung Rogers because he's in cahoots with Mallory?' The fury was beginning to show in Somers' expression as he asked for confirmation.

'That's about the size of it,' Dainton agreed. 'Still Dormer's not going to help Mallory any in the long run. We know Mallory's siding Willard now, so that makes it kinda legal to ventilate him when the chance comes.'

Rollo leaned his big, shaggy head over Somers' shoulder and gave Dainton a straight look. 'Jack Mallory and Des Willard will take some ventilating, Dainton,' he growled. 'You aiming on getting us to do the chore?'

Dainton's expression did not alter but he felt annoyance at the way Rollo had got to the nub of the scheme. 'Nobody does the chore for me, Rollo,' he replied smoothly. 'I've no more interest than seeing justice done for the killing of Jeff Willard an' Suter. If I was thinking of gunplay, then I can't think of anyone faster than me in Butane, but I don't aim to take on lawman's work on my lonesome.'

'How come you're so darned concerned with justice?' Rollo questioned. The Lazy Q cook had been hitting the bottle pretty hard and his tongue was getting freer rein than usual, but the gleam that shone deep in Dainton's eyes as he stared at Rollo chased away the effects of the spirit and he had the sense to temper the question with a grin.

'Like I said before, when the law catches up with Des Willard the Box Q belongs to me.' Dainton spoke evenly. 'But just because that's so, it's no reason for me to apologise to anyone for wanting to see a killer pay for his crimes.'

'Yeah, I guess you're right.' Rollo tried to look disarming, then turned away and devoted his attention to the floor-show girls, who had just made their appearance and were mingling around the saloon.

Although normally volatile, Ike Somers on this occasion kept his thoughts to himself; there was no percentage to be gained from allying himself to Dainton. A lot of men stayed close to Dainton and they always seemed to be well-heeled with dinero but they were men who had arrived at Butane with him. The more Somers gave his mind to things the more sure he became that his percentage lay in taking action himself and for himself. As Hubert Dainton made his unruffled way back to Slade's table, where Ezra Scott the banker now sat, he decided to pass on the details concerning Dormer to Hank Kershawe and Dan Smeaton. They could be trusted to shout for justice and, while they were fermenting the feelings of Butane folk and playing Dainton's game, he should have elbow-room to clean up the Box Q range of beef. Long before sundown Ike Somers and his men headed out of town.

Sitting at the same table with Ed Slade, Nolan and Creasey, Hubert Dainton noticed

Ike Somers and his men move out but he made nothing of it. He was pretty sure that Somers would fight shy now of burning down the Box Q. Maybe the Lazy Q man would run off enough steers to compensate him for the destruction of his own ranch-house but that was something that could be redressed soon enough. If Dainton's plans worked out, he would squeeze Ike Somers off the range in due course, so it did not matter two straws whether the beef was on Box Q or Lazy Q range.

When Manning came to the table later in the night Ed Slade stood up and, with a brief nod to Hubert Dainton, made his way out of the saloon. Manning watched him go, then sat down and helped himself to a drink out of Dainton's bottle. 'I never could see why you waste your time on that dried-up old windbag, he gives me the creeps.'

'The way he always moves off when you happen along it looks like you give him the creeps too.' There was a smile on Dainton's lips but there was no humour in his eyes. Manning shrugged the remark away but could not immediately shelve the fact that Dainton and Slade were so unlike that their friendship was surprising. As he downed his second drink he pushed the thought away by concluding that in some way or another Dainton found the old bank-teller useful. Never for one moment did it dawn on him that the boot was on the other foot.

As the night wore on, the war talk started up again, fomented by Hank Kershawe and Dan Smeaton. The word was bandied around that Willard and Mallory were at the Box Q and it was the duty of all right-minded Butane folk to see they were brought in to stand trial. Some men spoke of lynching but the memory of Dormer and his sidekick Amos Cotton was too green and the call for lynching was not taken up. Slim Manning sat drinking and eyeing the Maverick's newest dance hostesses with keen appreciation, entirely unmoved by the wild talk. It was Dainton who brought him alive to his responsibilities.

'These hombres could be in a mighty mean mood before this night's through, Slim,' he said quietly. 'I'm depending on you to see they don't set fire to the Box Q. When it comes to me I want it just the way it is.'

Manning nodded and after a long look at the new bottle Nolan had just brought to the table he circulated among the crowd, spreading words of caution.

Just before midnight, Squinty Robins pushed his way through the batwing doors and stared through the haze until he was able to pick out Dainton and his henchmen. He elbowed his way to the table and sat down in the chair Manning had vacated. Dainton stared at Squinty closely. The Box

Q cook was as pale as death and by the faraway look in his eyes had suffered one heck of a shock. When Dainton poured out a glass of bourbon and handed it across the table, Squinty's hand shook visibly. The sight of Squinty Robins spilling good liquor was too much for Nolan and he leaned across close to the cook.

'What in tarnation's the matter with you? Seen a ghost?'

Squinty tried hard to get both eyes focused on Nolan, then gave up. 'Yeah, I guess you could say that,' he answered as he turned his attention to Dainton. 'I've got something mighty important to say to you an' mebbe it's better for us to be on our own some place.'

'You can say anything you want in front of Nolan and Creasey, they've worked for me a long time, an' nobody else is going to hear with all this ruckus going on.'

Squinty looked doubtful, but he had gone through a very harrowing experience and he just had to talk about it in the hope of getting it out of his system. He leaned across the table and spoke in a hoarse whisper. 'Willard and Mallory are at the Box Q.' There was no reaction to that remark and Squinty felt a bit aggrieved but he went on. 'I heard them talking an' they're coming into town tonight to prove Willard didn't kill Suter.'

'And how're they going to do that?' Dainton's question came rapidly. Squinty had their attention now.

'Well, they're gonna demand that Suter's body is dug up an' for the doc to take the slug that killed him outa his carcass. I guess I'd forgotten, but when they mentioned the make of side-guns Willard totes I sure enough remembered, like all Butane folk will remember. Both Willards packed Adams guns an' the slugs are .38s.'

Dainton was staring hard into the middle distance and both Nolan and Creasey were breathing hard.

'They'll be backed by a dozen or so horse-herders an' by what I've seen of them nothing's gonna turn them aside when they set out to do something.'

'Well, what's this got to do with me?' Dainton asked. 'Seems to me it's Manning you want.' Squinty managed to keep two eyes aligned on Dainton for a couple of seconds and he was able to read the alarm that Dainton's wooden expression tried to mask.

'The way I heard Mallory and Willard talk, if no .38 is pulled outa Suter's body, then he was killed by one of you an' considering you're head man I reckoned I'd be doing you a favour by giving you the news.'

Dainton nodded slowly. It seemed the only way to deal with this situation would be to stir up enough feeling so that the townsfolk would take the initiative and string Willard and Mallory up despite Dormer's horse-herders. His mind ran on to the possibility of having Nolan and Creasey pick Willard and Mallory off with rifle fire from the rooftops, when the crowd started shouting for blood. He had to drag his thoughts back when Squinty went on talking.

'I figured if I made certain they'd find a .38 slug in the hole in Suter's chest then I'd be sure of a fair-sized handout from you.' Dainton was staring hard at Squinty now and Nolan and Creasey were both puzzled.

'Tell me,' Dainton breathed and Squinty went on.

'I took one of Jeff's guns and some shells an' on the way into town flattened a slug against a hunk of rock. I dug down to Suter's coffin and stashed the slug in the hole in his chest. I just finished covering him up again.'

A slow smile crossed Dainton's face, and his henchmen showed their relief in wide grins.

'That's sure some chore you set yourself on account of me, Squinty,' Dainton purred. 'Must have taken a lot of gall. Er, you still got that Adams six-shooter?'

Squinty's hand went inside his shirt and he took out the gun which was rolled in a bandanna. He passed it across the table, and Dainton transferred it inside his own shirt.

'They'd have found a .38 anyhow, Squinty,'

Dainton said evenly. 'We saw Willard shoot Suter down but I guess I owe you plenty for what you did on my account.' Dainton pulled out a roll of notes and peeled some off. These he passed to Squinty, who took them up eagerly enough. 'Maybe you'd better light outa town after the fun's over tonight; that way nobody's gonna find out what you did, and that being so, you'll need a whole lot more dinero.' Squinty's eyes were star-bright now.

'I was aiming to ride back to the Box Q,' he said. 'There ain't no call for me to ride into the sun.'

Dainton looked at him a long time before replying. 'That's so,' he said at length. 'Anyway's, it looks like the Box Q will be my spread pretty soon so you'll be on my payroll. When the fun's over tonight, just call at Ed Slade's and you'll get the rest that's due to you.' With a tight smile at Squinty, Hubert Dainton got up and pushed his way out into the night, leaving Nolan and Creasey to share in the drinking session the Box Q cook started out of his hard-earned wealth.

Chapter Five

Ed Slade surveyed his partner thoughtfully after Dainton had brought him up to date. 'That was sure good thinking on Squinty's part,' he said slowly. 'And it must have taken a lot of spunk to plant the evidence in Suter's corpse, but he didn't do it for you, he reckoned on a quick job with a good profit. What's the size of the handout you're reckoning on paying him?'

Dainton smiled as he reached across the table for the bottle that stood near Slade's elbow. 'Reckon I'll ply him in metal, mebbe a .38 slug.'

Slade's smile was full of approval, he had trained Dainton well. 'That's sense,' he agreed. 'His next quick profit could bring us grief.' There was a pause while both men took a gulp of bourbon, then Slade moved on to plans for the immediate future. Squinty's fate was already assured and he had no further mention. The long years of collaboration had resulted in a keen understanding between the two men and they sat relaxed, enjoying the smooth spirit and smoking cheroots while they waited for the crowd noises that would herald the arrival of Mallory and Willard. When the hubbub broke, they merely exchanged meaningful glances and Dainton took his leave just a minute or so ahead of Ed Slade.

Dainton moved easily along the sidewalk towards the huddle of men grouped around the jailhouse door. By the light thrown out of saloon windows each side of the street, he could make out about a dozen riders formed in a tight ring just beyond the jail and a couple of riders hemmed in by the ring. A lot of men stood a little way off from the riders and the names Willard and Mallory were being shouted to other men, who were pouring out of the saloons and dance-halls. As Dainton closed the distance he recognised Seth Dormer, Rogers and Amos Cotton haranguing Slim Manning.

'Willard's got a right to have his claim investigated,' Dormer was saying loudly as Dainton edged alongside Manning. 'And I'm telling you to arrange for the Doc to dig the slug that killed Sheriff Suter out of his corpse pronto. You all know what shooting irons the Willards used, so, by my reckoning, if the slug that's dug out is anything but a .38 then Willard's not guilty.' Manning was staring wild-eyed at Dormer and for once he had difficulty in formulating words. 'And if he's not guilty of killing Suter, then by my book, there's nothing to prove that he killed his brother. Maybe Suter's killer did that killing too.'

'You're forgetting, Dormer, I saw Willard kill Suter,' Slim Manning managed at last, 'An' Dainton did, an' three other hombres, so why in heck do we need to go along with this crazy notion?'

The shouts from the crowd held numerous threats to Mallory and Willard but the riders were unruffled. They all looked competent to deal with any situation that might boil up and Manning's hope of violent intervention saving the day faded, as he struggled for words.

'Can't see why you don't accommodate Dormer, Slim,' Hubert Dainton put in, the smile on his face was easy and Manning flashed a doubtful glance at him. At once he scented a double-cross. The other men present at the time of the killing were Dainton's men and, collectively, they could swear they had left him along with Suter after Willard's first shot had stunned the sheriff. Dainton's following words reassured him and the Butane deputy decided to go along with the request. 'I guess we all know that Des packs a couple of Adams shooting irons, an', like Manning said, we saw Des kill Suter.'

'Well?' Dormer's voice barked the question and Manning shrugged his shoulders.

'I'll get the doc,' he snarled. 'But I'll be durned if I'll give any help. If you hombres want Suter dug up you've got yourselves a chore. I'll see you at the funeral parlour.'

The word got around the crowd quickly and while there were no volunteers to help in the grisly work afoot, the majority of men were eager enough to follow the riders to Boot Hill.

Willard and Mallory sat their mounts apart from the crowd that gathered behind Dormer's men, who worked by the light of kerosene flares. Neither man spoke, their attention being rivetted on the men who piled spadeful after spadeful of loose earth beside the shallow grave. Willard was tense and eager for the chore to be completed so that he could take his place again among the folks who had been his friends, Mallory was full of unease. The way Dainton and Manning had agreed to have Suter's corpse examined and the cool way Dainton had come along in front of the crowd bothered him. He had difficulty stifling the doubts that kept crowding in.

Dormer's men made easy work of the chore and in a suprisingly short time the coffin was hauled out and carried to the funeral parlour. The crowd followed in sober silence. A lot of men were conscious that no matter what was at stake now, the body they followed was Sheriff Suter's and one thing was for sure, Suter had earned respect in his lifetime.

The big double doors of the funeral parlour were wide open and the room was well illuminated by three lamps suspended from beams near to the bare trestle-type table that was the sole article of furniture. Doc Colehan stood with Slim Manning and eyed the coffin balefully as it was lifted on to the table.

The bearers sought the fresh night air and rolled themselves cigarettes, but Dormer, Cotton, Rogers and Dainton stepped inside the funeral parlour. Mallory and Des Willard stayed outside, their mounts just beyond the range of light, Nolan and Creasey stood quite close to them but in the darkness, and both men had their hands on their shooting-irons.

A lot of men felt their skin prickling as the lid came off the coffin but Doc Colehan appeared unmoved, his burly figure blocked his movements from the crowd and the men inside the funeral parlour seemed in no haste to watch his handiwork closely. Dormer cast covert glances at Dainton and Slim Manning but Dainton appeared calm and unruffled, Manning was tense but Dormer reckoned there were normal reasons for that. Not everybody liked digging up the dead.

Doc Colehan took his time over his part in the proceedings. He moved back from the table to his bag of instruments a few times, pausing now and again to eye the men in the funeral parlour. He wanted them to get the full benefit from the chore so rudely thrust upon him, and also, if Suter had died from hands other than Des Willard's, he wanted the murderer or murderers so wrought up inside that the evidence, when presented, would render them a mite slow on the up-take. He had no desire to end up just yet on the funeral parlour table by stopping a stray bullet in the general mêlée.

The atmosphere in the inhospitable room became almost intolerable as the doc applied himself to the job with agonising slowness, and the perspiration gathered on Manning's forehead in huge globules that soon fur-rowed their way down his face. Only Dain-ton looked calm, and he whiled the time by rolling himself a smoke.

At long last Doc Colehan straightened and held out the forceps that held the slug he had drawn out of Suter's body. Seth Dormer held out his hand and the doc dropped the slug into it, then headed straight through the door to the mortician's office. Manning, Cotton and Dainton closed in on Dormer and stared hard at the slug.

'Well!' Dainton's face was bland as he stared at Dormer. 'That's no .45.' Dormer shook his head slowly.

'I guess not. That's a .38.'

As Dormer spoke, Slim Manning sprung to life, he pushed his way to the open door-way and staring out into the night, shouted. 'The doc dug a .38 slug outa Suter, so that proves you did the killing Willard like we said. I'm taking you in, hombre!'

In the split second before the crowd noises erupted, Des Willard scaled the whole range of thought processes from amazement to disbelief, he also divined in that instant that to keep a whole skin he had to move fast. His heels drummed into the palomino's flanks and the animal cannoned into Mallory's mount as Willard headed for the gap between the funeral parlour and the furniture store. Mallory's horse swung into Nolan and Creasey, who had intended to wing Willard, sending them reeling and cursing into the dust.

The crowd made plenty of noise but no one seemed in a hurry to set out after the fugitive and the fading hoofbeats became lost in the general hubbub. As Jack Mallory slid to the ground and pushed his way to the funeral parlour some townsfolk grabbed at him vengefully, but he jerked himself free and crossed the pool of light. Manning glared at him as he made the doorway. Dormer thrust his hand in front of Mallory and the horse-rancher stared unbelievingly at the slug that ended Suter's life.

'You still siding Willard, Mallory?' Manning's voice boomed so that everyone could hear, and the crowd went silent, waiting for the reply.

Jack Mallory felt physical revulsion as he

continued to stare at the .38 slug. He had been prepared to stake his life on Willard's assertion that he had only fired one shot at Suter. His thoughts slid around in a whirl as he shook his head. 'I guess not. Seems he made a fool outa me.'

Before Manning could make any scathing remark, Hubert Dainton pushed in front of him. Dainton's big face was contorted into what he hoped was a compassionate expression. 'I guess it's natural enough to take a pard's word against that of other folk, Mallory,' he said, loud enough for most of the crowd to hear. 'And I guess if you're convinced now young Des is a killer, we can all forget you took sides.'

The new-found knowledge that his life-long pardner was indeed a cold-blooded killer did not help him to take kindly to Dainton's claptrap. He just glared at the man and turning abruptly, left the building. Rogers followed his boss close, just in case some of the crowd did not go along with Dainton's peace talk, but he need not have worried, no one attempted to impede Mallory as he got to his horse and mounted. There was no urgency about Jack Mallory's departure and Rogers guessed that he was travelling no farther than the Maverick to swill away the years of memories that must be mocking him. Rogers stood and waited for Dormer and Cotton, but as they made to leave the building, Manning's sneering voice stayed them.

'You hombres ain't going any place until the chore is finished,' he shouted. 'The Sheriff needs burying again.'

Dormer's eyes sparked fire but he nodded and barked an order to his men. Half a dozen hands moved into the funeral parlour and, after refastening the lid of the coffin, returned into the night, bearing Suter's remains. When the crowd had moved away and just Dainton and Manning stood in the lighted doorway Dainton fixed Manning with hate-ridden eyes.

'Did you have to open your blamed mouth?' he snarled.

Manning stared at him in astonishment. 'What in heck's eating you?' he asked.

'Just a couple of minutes alone with Suter's body an' nobody or nothing could change the way things seem to add up. We'd have had Willard over a barrel for all time.'

'I – I don't get you,' the lawman stammered. 'I figured it was all squared anyway.'

'That .38 was planted,' Dainton breathed. 'But the blamed fool that planted it didn't take out the .45 that killed Suter.'

Manning shook his head in perplexity. 'I reckoned you had used a .38 smoke-pole when you killed Suter,' he muttered. 'That's why I figured you weren't worried any when they wanted Suter dug up.'

'Maybe it won't matter,' Dainton said at length. 'C'mon, let's go, the place gives me the creeps.'

As they stepped out of the range of light Dainton peeled off a few notes from his roll and stuffed them into Manning's hand. 'Considering all things, this night's work might have put us in the clear. I guess you can celebrate some, unless you're hankering after heading a posse after Willard.'

Manning chuckled in the dark, his humour restored by the crisp crackle of the folding money as he stuffed it into a vest pocket. 'He's not going to worry anybody hereabouts after tonight's showdown, so I guess I can leave it to some trigger-happy lawman to account for Willard some time.'

'Get his picture circulated with a reward caption big enough to get some bounty-hunters on his trail, make it dead or alive. Most bounty-hunters I've heard of make a quick kill – that way they don't lay up troubles for themselves on the way back.'

At the Maverick they parted company, Manning going inside to celebrate and Dainton on to Ed Slade's place and his subsequent meeting with Squinty Robins.

Des Willard pulled his palomino to a stop a couple of miles along the Alpine road, south of Butane, and strained his ears to pick up sounds of pursuit as he rolled himself a smoke. His mind was in a turmoil and he was beginning to believe that he had killed Suter. Dormer, Rogers and Doc Colehan had all seen the slug that the doc had taken out of the corpse and they had remained silent when Manning had made his statement. They were not likely to make a mistake, so he had to accept the fact that Suter had died from a .38 bullet, and he reluctantly admitted to himself that only he used guns that fired that calibre bullet.

As he drew the smoke deep into his lungs, drawing some solace from the strong tobacco, he searched his mind irresolutely for his next move. If he stayed near Butane, then, sooner or later, he would have to deal in death to keep out of the clutches of the law. No matter which way his thoughts skipped around the problem he could see no prospect of returning to a normal way of life. By this time, no doubt, those who had believed in him – Mallory, Dormer and the others – would be cursing themselves for fools and steeling themselves to become indifferent to his fate.

When his thoughts turned to Sal Dormer his inborn stubbornness pushed through. It mattered to him that the girl would hear from other sources that he was a murderer. He wanted to see how she looked when he told her again that, despite all the evidence, he had not killed Suter. What showed in her eyes would help him decide whether to stay around and fight back or take his chances over the skyline. Stubbing the cigarette out he turned the palomino around and headed back for Butane.

Des rode the couple of miles back at walking pace. If he was going to have to travel fast out of town, then he wanted his palomino in peak condition. He skirted the town wide, then rode in unerringly to the point between Ezra Scott's and Judge Carter's houses. Dismounting at the rear, he made his way cautiously to the front. There was plenty of noise going on in Butane but it came from the saloons much farther down Main Street. No one bothered to venture this far away from the centre of things, so Willard felt quite safe in knocking at the banker's door.

After a few seconds the door opened and Sheila Scott peered out at him. There was hardly any light in the hallway, only the strip of light that escaped from the inner room door which she had left nearly closed, but she recognised him immediately. 'Des,' she whispered. 'What do you want here? I thought you'd be getting as far from Butane as possible.'

Willard did not answer and, as footsteps sounded coming up Main Street, he swivelled his head and waited, tense.

'You'd better come inside,' Sheila said, and stood aside to let him in.

He followed her into the drawing-room and stood at the door irresolute, conscious of the cool brown eyes appraising him from beside the fireplace. For a moment he was unaware of Sheila Scott beside him and of the rest of his surroundings. He stood caught in the spell of Sal Dormer's beauty. She had changed out of range clothes and wore a jade-green dress that complemented her hair and colouring to perfection and gave subtle accent to her exquisite figure. There was no smile on her face and her eyes were serious.

'You'd best sit down,' Sheila Scott remarked, bringing him back to earth. 'And I'll get you a drink.'

Des nodded, and stepped across the room to the large leather armchair opposite the fireplace. He placed his sombrero on the floor beside him as Sheila handed him a glass of bourbon. 'Thanks, I can certainly do with this.' He took a sip and looked down into the glass, his face set. 'Things have sure become involved, and just when I reckoned they were going to work out.'

'I guess if you kill a lawman you can expect to get involved,' Sheila said unsteadily and Des stared up at her with red blood darkening his face. He bit back the words that rushed to his lips. 'We've heard the bullet that killed Sheriff Suter was from a gun you carry, Des, so what can you expect us to believe? You've admitted to having aimed and fired at him.'

'Maybe now I'll never be able to prove what I say.' Des remarked, and he looked the girls straight in the face one after the other. 'But things happened the way I said – I didn't kill Suter. With the evidence stacked the way it is I can't expect any support from my enemies. I reckoned on some from my friends.'

'Just what can you expect?' Sheila asked. 'They were ready to help and believe until tonight. As much as we want to believe, I'm afraid we can't.'

Willard's face was serious as he nodded his understanding. He stood up slowly, picking up his sombrero as he did so. 'And your father, what does he think?' he set considerable store on Ezra Scott.

'He didn't say,' Sheila replied. 'He's gone back to the bank.'

'Well, I guess I'd better ride into the sun and forget Butane. Maybe some time the truth will come out.'

Willard was about to go when Sal Dormer moved from her place beside the wide mantelshelf and came towards him. Her eyes had softened and he felt a lump in his throat as he looked at her.

'Leaving the territory may be a good idea,' she said. 'But you can travel knowing I believe you're innocent. Your word's good enough for me.'

The worry lines disappeared like magic from Willard's face and his lips split into the wide smile that Sal had found so fascinating the first time. 'I'm sure glad you believe me, Miss Sal,' he said quietly. 'I'll ride a lot easier in mind on that account and maybe I won't ride so far after all. If the rest of my friends doubt my innocence, then it looks like I'll have to stay close enough to dig out the truth myself.'

The smile Sal Dormer gave him sent Des Willard out of Ezra Scott's with the weight lifted from his shoulders. He did not try to analyse the reasons for the girl's belief in him. At this moment it was enough that she had announced her belief. He moved around the building with a light and carefree step to where he had left the palomino, and as his mount cleared the southern limits of the town the girl's smile remained in his mind's eye, cheering him, brightening the way.

Squinty Robins saw Dainton and Slim Manning part company outside the Maverick and, after using up about ten minutes with a couple of drinks in the Longhorn, he made his way to keep his appointment with Dainton. Squinty felt good. The work he had put in earlier in the night had paid off handsomely with Dainton. Despite Dainton's insistence that Willard had in fact shot Suter,

Squinty was not fooled any and he reckoned that the handout he'd get would be mighty big.

Ed Slade's house was on the edge of Main Street, just a stone's throw from the livery stable, and set back behind a tall creosoted fence. Squinty stood at the gateway and peered into the darkness over the gate. No vestige of light reached from the saloons and dance-halls and suddenly the Box Q cook felt lonely. Goose-pimples stood out on his skin and a chill entered his blood. Then suddenly Dainton's big form was beside him and the man's soothing, urbane words chased the fears away.

'Mighty glad you made it on time, Squinty, come right on inside. Ed and me are in cahoots so he knows the score.'

'Sure thing, Dainton, lead the way.' The eagerness was back in Squinty now.

Dainton led Squinty up the pathway, into the house and through the hall into the living-room. Ed Slade looked up at him with as much enthusiasm as his desiccated countenance could muster and waved him to a seat at the opposite side of the table. Hubert Dainton moved a chair beside Squinty and eased himself into it like an amiable bear.

'Howdy, Ed,' Squinty said. 'I didn't know you an' Dainton was pardners.'

'I guess it won't matter much you knowing

Squinty,' Slade said easily. 'It looks like you're plumb on our side.' The Box Q cook's head nodded vigorously. 'That was mighty good work you did tonight,' Slade continued. 'Shows you've got a lot of good sense.'

'Well, I figured I could do Dainton a bit of good an' it sure panned out that way.' Squinty was keen to add to the ante. 'Reckon what I did is worth a fair stack of dinero.'

'That's the way we figure too, Squinty,' Dainton murmured as he poured out three drinks and passed two to the other men.

Ed Slade reached into a drawer and, after pulling out the Adams six-shooter, placed it in front of him. 'You were sure lucky to get hold of this, sort of clinched things for us.'

Squinty's spirits soared rapidly. His thoughts were running ahead and he could almost feel the thick roll of notes pressing against his chest from his inside pocket. His eyes followed each other to the pile of money that Slade pulled out of the drawer and laid on the table. It took him a few moments to swivel his attention from the money to the next item Slade laid on the table and for a moment its purpose escaped him. It was a wide section of blanket that Slade proceeded to fold. Squinty was just thinking there was no need for Slade to wrap the money in the blanket when the awful truth dawned.

At the precise moment, the cold muzzle of the gun Dainton had palmed was pressed into Squinty's temple and he stared in horrible fascination as Slade wrapped the thickly folded blanket around the barrel of the Adams .38. There was keen enjoyment on Ed Slade's face as he watched Squinty's expression change from surprise to crawling fear, so he took his time.

'Y'know, Squinty,' he drawled. 'We'd have liked fine to give you a proper reward for what you did but I guess you understand there'd always be a temptation to spill what you know to Mallory or some lawman if you run short of dinero.' The conversation was going over Squinty's head, he was staring at the blanketed gun mesmerised. The stress of the moment had even corrected the misalignment of his eyes. 'Considering you're the only hombre who can put the heat on us we'd be plum foolish not to deal with you.'

The blanketed gun came up as Slade spoke and suddenly the scales of fear fell away from Squinty's mind. His arm next to Dainton flew up, knocking away the hand that held the gun to his temple, then he was falling backwards, taking his chair with him as he clawed with his right hand for a gun. Neither Dainton nor Slade spoke, Dainton had not intended using his gun anyway. As Squinty went backwards so Slade rose up from the table, following the little cook's progress. He fired just as Squinty's gun cleared leather and, straightaway, the cook's gun dropped from nerveless fingers beside his apparently lifeless body.

Dainton and his henchman glanced at one another in grim satisfaction, and Dainton picked up the fallen chair and returned it to its previous position before resuming his seat. Slade laid the Adams .38 on the table and refilled two glasses with bourbon. Squinty's body cast no shadow upon their enjoyment as the two men drank to the success of their plans.

'Ezra Scott should be just about through with that consignment for the stage-run by now.' Slade remarked at length. 'So I guess it's time I paid him a visit.' He gave a hard laugh. 'Willard's going to have a whole lot to answer for by the time the law catches up with him.'

Dainton nodded, a far-away look in his eyes. 'Yeah, I guess we've cooked his goose. Maybe I'll let Mallory know I'm taking over the Box Q right away. He was mighty sick at the way he opined Willard had fooled him and I'm not thinking he'll make any attempt to hold on to the spread for his pard.' Hubert Dainton paused and took another drink. 'It could be that Ike Somers will try throwing a loop over some Box Q beef to-night, so if I ride in to take over, maybe I can take care of that problem nice and legally.'

'You might get trouble with Dan Smeaton and Hank Kershawe, they've been mighty close to Somers for some time.'

Dainton shrugged Slade's warning away. 'We'll let Slim Manning earn his keep. Maybe after tonight we'll need this town to be law-abiding, so he can start in on Smeaton and Kershawe if they belly-ache too much.'

They left the house together, but Dainton waited inside the fence for Slade to get well on his way to the bank before heading for the Maverick. He permitted himself a wide smile of satisfaction in the dark.

Chapter Six

It took half a bottle of bourbon to temper the shock Mallory had received that night. Dormer, Cotton and Mike Rogers left him to his brooding. They realised that no amount of talk from them would help him. He had to sort out his own feelings about Willard and decide his own future actions. Dormer had called at the banker's house to give the news to Sal and Sheila Scott and had been shocked by the way the news affected his daughter. Now, as he watched Mallory square his shoulders and turn away from the bar, he concluded that the sooner he and his men moved out of Butane the better. It seemed to him that Sal had developed a great liking for Willard in the short time they had known each other, and remaining in Butane would only tend to aggravate her sorrow at finding Willard to be a killer.

Mallory pulled a chair from beside another table and sat down beside Mike Rogers, who poured out a drink and pushed it along the table. Seth Dormer leaned across the table, catching Mallory's eye.

'I've got a notion we should get back to the Box Q and settle up our affairs. It could be the wolves will be muscling in on the stock tonight, because the way it looks, Willard's never going to stake a claim on the spread again, and maybe a lot of folk are thinking it's every man for himself.'

'Yeah, sure.' Mallory's reply was laconic. It seemed he was not too concerned whether Willard came back or not. He took time to roll himself a smoke and Dormer could see he was struggling to throw off his disappointment and shock to concentrate on the needs of the moment. The Triple Bar man was halfway through the cigarette when Hubert Dainton entered the saloon and, after having located the table through the pall of smoke, made his way smoothly to Mallory's side. Pulling a chair from beside another table he sat down. Grudgingly Mallory pushed a glass and the bottle towards him.

'I thought I'd let you know Mallory I'm taking over the Box Q as of now.' Dainton managed to convey regret in his voice, as though the spread would be an encumbrance to him. 'There's no sense in holding off until some lawman or bounty-hunter gets Des in his sights – that way I'm going to be out a lot of stock. If he comes back some time and the law gives him a jail sentence, then I guess I'll hand it back on a plate to him when he's ready.'

Mallory glared a bit as he surveyed Dainton. The man's easy talk fooled him none.

Dainton had got what he had been after. Maybe Des had allowed the ranch to fall into his uncle's hands but somehow Mallory reckoned the circumstances had been engineered by Dainton. Legally Dainton was on safe ground, being the next-of-kin to Des Willard, and he had every right to keep a close watch on Box Q stock and property. Mallory had run clean dry of argument and he shrugged his shoulders, making no comment. Seth Dormer took up the conversation.

'We'll ride along with you, Dainton,' he said decisively. 'I've got a mighty large string of horseflesh grazing on the Box Q with Willard's permission. I guess we'll be moving 'em outa the territory.'

Dainton's smile was benign as he reached for the bottle. 'Just as you want, Dormer,' he replied. 'You're welcome to let 'em graze until you're good and ready.'

'I'm obliged to you, Dainton, but there's nothing to keep us in this neck of the hills now; we'll move 'em out at sun-up.'

Hubert Dainton nodded and, drinking off what remained in his glass, made his way to where Nolan and Creasey were sat huddled close with two heavy bosomed members of the floor-show.

'He sure is upset at taking over the Box Q,' Mike Rogers remarked sarcastically and Mallory gave him a sour look.

'You know something,' Abe Cotton chipped in, his eyes on Dainton and his men. 'The more I see of that hombre, his sidekicks an' the lawman, the more convinced I get that young Willard's on the receiving end of a deep plot.'

Cotton was not given to much talk and through the years Dormer had learned to take notice when his scout made any observation. Mallory looked across the table, an astonished expression on his face.

'It just doesn't add up to me how a spread falls into the hands of a hombre like Dainton so nice and easy. How come he and his men formed the posse that trailed Willard? Has he always been so hot in upholding the law?'

Mallory shook his head. 'No, I'm thinking he joined up with the sheriff and the deputy in the hope of putting a slug into Des. The way things have worked out he gets the spread the easy way.'

'Well, Abe, things mostly prove you right, but I'm not forgetting that none of the fellers who swear Willard killed Suter were worried any when we got the doc to dig out the slug.' Dormer remarked.

'That Deputy Manning was worried plenty until Dainton came along,' Cotton contradicted. 'Anyways, no matter what the evidence says, I still think Willard's innocent.'

A few minutes later Hubert Dainton made his way back to their table, followed by

Nolan and Creasey. He paused briefly and gave them all the benefit of his benign smile. 'We're making for the Box Q as soon as Nolan collects the rest of my outfit. If you ride along it could save accidents later.'

'How come accidents?' Mallory growled. Dainton's smile widened.

'Well, I'm not aiming on letting much free movement over Box Q territory after I take over. It could be some of my men would shoot first and ask questions after.'

Mallory stood up and stared hard into Dainton's face. 'If we're all going to get trigger-happy on this range, then don't ever forget you're starting it and remember it's not always the most guns that count.'

Dainton's expression did not alter but his eyes held a deep mocking quality. He shrugged his heavy shoulders dispassionately. 'Who's talking about a range war?' he asked easily. 'All I'm saying is, that my men will be keeping folk off Box Q range. A man's got a right to say who crosses his line.'

Mallory looked as though he would carry the verbal battle on a stage farther but he thought better of it and nodded to Mike Rogers as Dainton moved out on to the sidewalk. 'Let's get moving, then.'

As Mike Rogers pushed his chair away and stood up to follow his boss out of the saloon, Dormer and Cotton exchanged significant glances.

'The usual pattern, Abe,' Dormer remarked quietly. 'The Big Man starting to take over, calling the tune. Dainton's got the law in his pocket and now owns the biggest spread. He'll drop the good-natured pose mighty soon now and make it obvious to everyone he's king.'

'Huh – it's happening everywhere,' Cotton grumbled as he stood up. 'If we stop off to fight every range-hog we'll never get the cayuses to the end of the trail.'

Dormer's eyes glinted with humour as he flashed a glance at his scout. He knew Cotton had already divined his intention to stay behind whilst Abe pushed on with the horse-herd and he reckoned Abe wanted this particular cattle-king cut down to size. 'I'd already thought along those lines, Abe,' he replied as he pushed his chair away and headed for the door, 'So I guess you'd better push on with the broncs. I'll stay on a bit and see how things develop.'

Cotton turned to glare at him but Dormer affected not to see and they joined Mallory and Mike Rogers on the sidewalk. About ten minutes later they rode out of Butane behind Hubert Dainton's hard-faced crew en route for the Box Q.

Des Willard rode along for a couple of hours with no fixed purpose in mind. In point of fact his thoughts remained on the same uplifting theme, the expression of belief in his innocence by Sal Dormer. The picture of her remained in his mind's eye and his pulse quickened again and again as he remembered the earnest expression on her lovely face. It was good to know such a woman believed in him. The thought flitted through his mind for the hundredth time, then he drew his palomino to a stop as his thoughts ran on. All the time he had been heading south, keeping close to the Alpine trail and, although he would not have admitted as much, instinctively his direction was towards the not too distant Rio Grande and Mexico, beyond the reach of Texan lawmen.

It would be no satisfaction to him in years to come somewhere in Mexico to reflect that Sal Dormer had believed in him. He had to prove his innocence here and now so that he could share the future with the girl. Sooner or later, if he kept moving, he would be driven to survive by the speed of his gun and innocent people might fall to him. Back in Butane there were men who deserved to die at his hands, so Butane was the place that should have the benefit of his undoubted skill with his six-guns.

With the decision made Willard turned his palomino around and gigged the animal into a steady canter. He now knew where he wanted to be. There were a couple of apparently blind canyons quite close to one of the

Box Q line-shacks but he knew how to move in and out of them at will. He reckoned he would keep himself under cover there until it suited his book to make his presence felt.

His spirits lightened as his palomino's lengthy strides took him back towards Butane. He even grinned as he contemplated taking the fight to his enemies, and later as he skirted Butane and joined the north trail towards the Box Q he gave consideration to the men who alleged they had witnessed the killing of Sheriff Suter. The weakest link he wanted, the one most likely to back down and spill the truth to save his own skin, but the more he considered Dainton, Manning, Nolan, Creasey and Tyler, the more doubtful he became that any of them would break down easily. He would need a lot of luck, Des reflected, the bitterness seeping back into his soul. The luck was waiting for him, but when it turned up it was hardly recognisable as such.

Just a mile or so beyond the fork that led to Ike Somers' Lazy Q spread Des picked up the sounds of steady hoofbeats ahead and, cutting down his mount's pace to suit the speed of the horsemen in front, peered intently through the gloom. The moon had just edged over the skyline but as yet it had not gained sufficient height to spread any effective light, so it took a couple of minutes careful riding before he made out the moving area of deeper black in the general gloom ahead of him. It seemed to Des Willard that there was something wrong about the shape of the blurred patch for it to be a horse and rider, then suddenly he understood and pushed the palomino forward at a faster gait.

Before he drew alongside the animal he had made out the figure of the rider slumped over the saddle pommel but recognition did not come until he pulled the horse to a stop. Sliding to the ground, Des raised the man's head from where it rested against the animal's neck and he whistled his surprise. 'Squinty Robins,' he muttered. 'Now what in heck's happened to him?'

Leading both horses off the trail, Des eased Squinty down to the ground. There was a lot of blood on the saddle, and the little cook's vest and shirt had reached such a state of saturation that Willard marvelled a man could lose so much blood and still live. He detected the faintest movement in the man's pulse but he reckoned Squinty's chance of survival was slight. One thing was certain, there was so little likelihood of the cook recovering that it was hardly worth risking his neck taking Squinty into Butane for medical attention.

Taking his medicine pack out of his saddle-roll, Des fixed a pad to the gaping wound in Squinty's chest and tied a tight bandage around him to keep the pad in place, then as gently as possible he draped the cook over his saddle and fastened him down so that he would ride as comfortably as possible. Willard remounted after fastening the lead rein to his own saddle cantle and set his palomino at a pace that would cause Squinty the least inconvenience.

When at length he came to the fork leading to the Box Q, Des struck across country to the north-west where a line-shack stood near to the blind canyon. The moon strengthened as it climbed the heavens, and the youngster had to use a lot of trail sense to keep moving without presenting himself and the led horse with its burden as easy targets for some trigger-happy night-rider, not that he expected anybody to be abroad zealously guarding his cattle. With Genner and his followers gone, there was no one left to take over that chore. Now and again he passed quite close to a group of steers bearing the Box Q brand but he saw no one until with the line-shack no more than half a mile distant, he saw, etched briefly upon the skyline, a dozen or more riders travelling fast.

There was little danger of any of them catching sight of him because at that moment he was passing behind a sparse clump of chaparral but his impulse was to throw caution to the wind and ride out after the horsemen to see for himself just what they were doing on his range, not that he had much doubt as to their intentions. His blood boiled as he pictured the riders rounding up group after group of sleek cattle and heading for Sedalia with a fortune at the end of the drive – his fortune – but he forced himself to ride on, away from the cover of the chaparral and on to the temporary shelter of the line-shack.

He had just pulled his mount to a halt in the shadow of the line-shack when a fusillade of shots rang out from the direction the riders had taken. Des scratched his head in perplexity as he slid to the ground. The intensity of the shooting increased and it was apparent to him that warring factions had joined forces somewhere over the ridge and were shooting in deadly earnest. He smiled grimly as he concluded there was no one out there shooting on his behalf, just two gangs of rustlers disputing ownership.

There was nothing Des could do about things, so he hauled Squinty down from his horse and, leaving the animals ground hitched, carried the cook into the hut. The moon shone with sufficient light through the dust-covered window to show him the bunk and, as gently as possible, he laid Squinty down. After covering up the window with a couple of blankets, Des lit up the oil-lamp that stood on the rough-hewn table. Then, forcing himself to ignore the increasing rate of fire in the distance, he undid the bandage and examined the little cook's wound.

The blood had stopped flowing but Des suspected that Squinty had none left to flow as he studied the size of the wound. He extracted a metal tobacco box out of the cook's vest pocket and as he saw the gouged and twisted lid he understood the reason for the jagged wound. The bullet had been deflected and had entered Squinty's body at an angle. He reckoned that the box could have saved the man's life if medical attention had been readily available, but he doubted whether it would make any difference now.

There was half a bottle of bourbon in the cupboard and Des allowed a trickle of the liquid to enter Squinty's mouth, but with no apparent result. Then he poured a drop into the wound to cauterise it before probing for the bullet. He was conscious of the drumming of hooves as he peered into the wound, and the thought registered that the firing had sent his cattle into a headlong stampede. They were heading for the line-shack, as far as he could judge, but with the steep-sided mountains just a couple of hundred yards or so to the west of the shack he reckoned the lead steers would change direction without involving him. The firing, too, had lessened in intensity but had steadied into something relentless and bitter, and every second it came closer.

He found the bullet and manoeuvred it out from between Squinty's breastbone and spare-rib, using his long-bladed knife, then, as he replaced the pad and refastened the bandage, he felt the shack shake as the herd thundered past no more than a hundred yards distant. The horsemen passed close, firing as they went. Just the briefest space of time passed before the next cavalcade of riders thundered by in pursuit. It seemed to him that even more men were shooting farther away to the east.

As he studied under the lamplight the bullet he had extracted from Squinty he thought bitterly that this was what folk had been after from the start, the chance to carve up the Box Q and cash in on a quick steal after discrediting the owner. Now, if Suter had still been around, the range would have been safe, but Suter was dead and he, Des Willard, had been framed for the killing. His mouth tightened in a hard line as the calibre of the bullet became evident. Squinty too, had been shot with a .38. It looked as if he was being lined up for this shooting as well.

He returned to the little cook's side and trickled a few more drops of bourbon into his mouth. Once again there was no apparent swallowing action but Squinty's pulse-beat became a little stronger. The man's face was deathly pale and, although Des had never particularly liked the Box Q cook, he felt some compassion for the man. He would have liked to have means available to give the man a chance of life. Then, as the implications of the .38 bullet sunk home, the need to keep Squinty alive became imperative. If only Squinty could recover to the extent of talking, then the identity would be revealed of the man who used a .38. Squinty must be kept alive and in the meantime kept out of sight. This posed quite a problem. It was extremely doubtful that the man would improve to the point of talking if he remained in the rugged comfort of the line-shack, but, if in order to keep him under cover, he were moved to the blind canyon where Des had been headed, then he could hardly survive.

Des scowled deeply in thought as the firing in the distance steadied. It sounded as though the men had stopped riding and were now battling from cover. He knew it was only a question of time before someone would halt at the line-shack, so the only thing to do was move the Box Q cook out and hope for a miracle.

Taking a moderate drink out of the bottle, Des then searched in the cupboards for supplies. He was well rewarded. It had always been the Box Q policy to keep the line-shacks well stocked and no one had made in-roads upon the provisions since the last topping up session. He filled a pair of leather aparajos with tinned foods, flour, sugar and coffee, and carrying them outside, fastened them to his palomino.

At the door of the shack he paused before re-entering and stared into the night in the direction of the firing. Beyond catching sight of the occasional stab of flame, the search was unproductive and with a shrug he turned to go back inside. Then above the staccato gun reports he picked up the hoofbeats of a single horse, travelling towards him at speed. He lost no time in entering the shack and, after extinguishing the oil-lamp, took up his position alongside the door.

As the hoofbeats sounded closer so the speed slackened, and Des knew for certain that the rider was headed for the shack. His face set into grim lines. The time had come to fight back. It looked as though in Butane the law was taking a holiday, particularly on his range, so it was time he stood four square and played his skill with his six-guns against the factions now decimating his stock. Bitterness crept into his soul as the rider drew to a stop outside the line-shack and at last he was ready to trade lead with anyone who fancied trying to take him in.

Ike Somers with Rollo, Mathers and the heavily bandaged Starr riding ahead of his crew approached the Box Q herd just when the animals were set on the move by Sam Genner and his side-kicks and only moments before the arrival of Dainton's outfit led to the outbreak of heavy gunfire.

Somers sent his men to head off the now maddened, thundering cattle, his first thoughts being to fight for as many beasts as he could head away, but there were too many men trading lead for his liking and he dropped back to shelter behind a huge rock at the edge of the steep mountain. His men were too far ahead to pull out now, and they would have to take their chances between the herd cutting close to the mountain's edge and the rival factions locked in deadly battle. His mind centred on the Box Q line-shack and the stock of bourbon that Jeff Willard had always kept there, and after giving the herd and the warring bands time to get clear, he moved his mount away from cover and set it to a run towards the line-shack.

Chapter Seven

Des Willard recognised the Lazy Q boss the moment the man stepped over the threshold and any regret he might have felt at what must happen drained away. Somers was a loud-mouth who had always been on the make and only Suter's iron hand had kept his avarice within bounds. The ownerless Box Q was a heaven-sent opportunity for Somers to feather his nest. The man paused, suddenly on guard as the acrid fumes from the extinguished kerosene lamp assailed his nostrils. His eyes rested briefly on the bunk, then swivelled around the room. Willard eased away from the wall and recognition brought a sharp hiss from the Lazy Q man.

'Willard!' Surprise showed through in the quality of Somers' tone but there was no trace of fear. He reckoned his chances against the younger man rated high enough to warrant confidence.

'Come right on in, Somers, and if you want to keep on living keep away from the hardware,' Ike Somers snorted derisively and moved into the centre of the shack.

'You're calling no tunes, Willard,' he snarled. 'Just button your lip and maybe I'll not run you into town.' He reached for the bottle of bourbon, then froze as Willard's voice imparted a menace that chilled him.

'Keep your thieving hands away from that bottle, Somers. Maybe the pace got a bit too hot for you out there, but you're not swilling my liquor while your men die doing your dirty work.'

Somers stared hard at Willard but the light was insufficient for him to make out more than the white blur of the younger man's face. He wondered just how much the other man knew. Willard enlightened him by continuing.

'You and the carrion you call a crew have tried rustling my beef and that gives me the right to shoot you down like the dog you are. I'm aiming to do just that but I'm giving you the chance to go for your shooting irons.'

'Your beef!' Somers spat the words out. 'You've got no claims on anything in this territory, Willard, an' it's nothing to you who takes Box Q beef.' The need for a drink was an overpowering temptation for him to dispatch Willard with the utmost speed and his confidence flowed back. He reached tentatively again for the bottle, taking Willard's attention from his other hand, which his body shielded. The gun cleared leather as he half turned to blast a couple of shots at the other man. The fraction of time that gave Willard his warning was immeasurable, but even as flame stabbed from Somers' gun, Des leapt aside. He felt the tug of the bullet that seared his side before thudding into the timbers, then as he clawed for his guns he sprawled over a chair Somers had kicked towards him. Two more bullets buried themselves deep into the floorboards as he rolled over and over. The wall brought him to a stop and he fired just once, aiming a little to the left and just a bit above the last gush of flame. He heard Somers gasp and choke on blood, then the man's gun clattered to the ground and, although it was only a second or so before the Lazy Q man pitched forward, it seemed to Des like all eternity.

Slowly Willard got up and crossed to Somers' side. The man was dead, exceedingly so, and Willard felt no remorse. It had been a close call but at least Somers had taught him one thing, when the chips were down, give your opponent a hundred per cent attention. As the long graze in his side made itself felt he reckoned he was lucky to have emerged with a salutary lesson.

There was nothing he could do for Somers and, after satisfying himself that the man had carried 45s, he set about moving Squinty Robins to his waiting horse. A couple of minutes later he headed away from the lineshack and, within the hour, he had Robins stretched out under the cover of an overhang in a blind canyon. The man's pulse still moved but so imperceptibly that it took Des about five minutes to convince himself that Squinty still lived.

Once again he allowed a trickle of bourbon to slide down the man's throat, then he gathered enough brushwood to start a fire. It was unlikely that anyone roaming his range this night knew of the existence of the canyon and the smoke funnelled straight up the sheer mountain wall so the fire would not give their hideout away. When he was certain that Squinty was as comfortable as possible Des remounted his palomino and, having gained level ground via the tortuous narrow defile, gave the animal its head after setting direction for Butane.

The firing had ceased but the fact merely registered in Willard's mind, he had probably lost his herd anyway. All it meant was that one gang of predators had beaten the other. He reckoned his beef was on the way to Sedalia now. He shrugged the thought away, it was enough to deal with one problem at a time and his current problem was to keep Robins alive. As he fastened his slicker against the icy wind he tried to analyse his reasons for riding into town. He had a hazy belief that Squinty Robins needed a womans' nursing to stand a chance but the thought had only germinated from his overwhelming desire to see more of Sal Dormer. Somehow, although their acquaintance was small, he felt convinced that she would help him and he coaxed more speed out of his mount so that he could put his belief to the test.

Des met no one on the ride into Butane but, when the little township was a quarter of a mile distant, he guided his palomino off the trail and made a wide detour, intent upon emerging between the stage-line compound and the blacksmith's forge. He tethered his mount to the top rail of the compound and made his way cautiously to Main Street. Lights showed in one of the saloons where the women augmented their floor-show earnings by bestowing their favours on men with the deepest purses, but mostly Butane had settled down for the night. Des turned left and, keeping to the shadow of the frame buildings, made his way towards Ezra Scott's house.

He was directly opposite the house when he saw the door open and, framed in the light from inside, were Slim Manning and Ed Slade. They paused a while at the doorway and Des had a momentary glimpse of a woman's dress beyond them. His curiosity mounted – there must be a pretty strong reason for Sheila Scott to be up at this time of night. Whatever the reason, he was relieved. He had expected having to get her and Sal Dormer out of bed. The feeling of relief vanished when, just after Manning and Slade headed for the jailhouse, Doc

121

Colehan came out of the Scott's house. Doc Colehan at this time of night meant trouble and his first thoughts were that something had happened to Sal.

When Colehan's footsteps faded, Des darted across the dusty roadway and, making the cover of the Scott's porch, tapped gently on the knocker. He was just debating whether or not to give another knock when the door opened and Sheila Scott's tear-stained face stared up at him an expression of surprise and anger upon it. She went to shut the door then thought better of it and Des stepped inside, pushing the door shut behind him. Sheila Scott fell away from him and stared at him from beside the hallstand.

'Why did you do it?' her voice was strained and hoarse. The door beside her opened and Sal Dormer glanced from one to the other, compassion for Sheila on her face. 'Why did you have to kill him?'

Des Willard stared, momentarily non-plussed. He shook his head uncertainly. 'I've told you before, Sheila. I didn't kill Suter,' he said quietly.

'You know I don't mean Suter.' There was an hysterical note in her voice now. 'What did my father do to you that you had to kill him?' she cried.

'Your father!' He stepped towards her involuntarily but her hands came up as though to push him away.

122

'Don't try to lie your way out of this, Des Willard,' she went on. 'Doc Colehan told me my father was killed by a .38 bullet.'

'I – I didn't know, Sheila,' Des stammered. 'I didn't do it. How in Hades could I do a thing like that to your father?'

The girl's eyes blazed suddenly and she raised the lid of the glove compartment in the hallstand and her hand came away holding a heavy, evil-looking .45. She held it as steady as a rock with the muzzle pointing to Willard's stomach.

'You killed your own brother.' She spat the words venomously. 'And the sheriff, and now my father. You've lied all the way and now I'm going to see you get what you deserve.'

Willard's face went suddenly cold. 'I'll tell you once again, Sheila, I did not kill Jeff or Suter, and the first I knew of your father's death is when you told me now. I came here in the hope of getting some help to nurse a man who's pretty near to death but I guess you've got troubles enough. If you want to fire that gun, go right ahead but you'll kill the wrong man.'

For a long moment it looked as though Sheila would pull the trigger. Her fingers whitened a little as it tightened against the pressure of the spring and Sal Dormer moved to her side with the speed of light, but before a restraining hand was placed on her arm the doubts had crowded back into

Sheila's mind and the pressure on the trigger relaxed. She allowed her hand to drop to her side. 'Just get out, Des Willard!' She said bitterly. 'I – I just don't know what to believe.' Abruptly Sheila Scott turned away and went through the doorway into the living-room, nearly closing the door behind her.

Des allowed his pent-up breath to escape in a sigh and his glance at Sal Dormer contained an expression of hopelessness. At every turn he came up against new problems and a mounting list of crimes laid at his door. The girl's quiet smile reassured him.

'You were saying you needed help for a wounded man?' Her matter-of-fact tone reassured him further. He nodded.

'Yeah. Another hombre with a .38 slug in him. I guess if he lives I'll know just who besides me carries a .38 gun.'

'What about Doc Colehan? Will he help?' Sal asked.

'I can't take the risk,' Des replied quickly. 'The doc'll most likely have him brought in an' if the ride doesn't kill him, then maybe the man who plugged him will get another chance before he talks. Nope!' Des shook his head decisively. 'I've got to try to keep him alive without spreading the news.'

Sal nodded her understanding and, catching a clear view of his profile in the line of light from the inside room, felt a rush of desire to help him. 'Tell me where to make for,' she said quietly. 'I can't leave before sun-up. There's not much of the night left but I guess it'll take some getting through for Sheila, and she needs a woman's company.'

Des outlined some topographical features of the range beyond the first fork of the north trail and Sal Dormer nodded readily enough. 'I'll be looking out for you – and thanks.' Des held out his hand involuntarily and the girl's smaller hand gripped his with a cool firmness. The brief touch affected both of them the same way and they parted company with hearts pounding and nerves a-tingle.

A couple of hours after sun-up, Des lay at full length at the brow of a smooth-topped hill watching Seth Dormer's horse-herd stream past down below towards Butane. Dormer rode ahead, tall in the saddle and beside him Jack Mallory rode hunch-shouldered. Des recognised Abe Cotton, who was haranguing a thick-chested rider on the right flank of the herd, and some of the herders who had ridden into Butane with him an age ago. He saw Sal Dormer round a bluff about a mile ahead of the horse herd. Then, obviously having seen the herd, she turned and moved back out of view. It was apparent that neither Seth Dormer nor Jack Mallory had seen her but, as Des took in the terrain ahead of the herd, he appreciated that Sal had merely seen the dust cloud that spilled upwards to the cloudless sky, and made her own assessment of the situation.

The herd moved on and streamed through the gap between the twin hills that rolled south-east and flattened themselves into the rolling grassland beside the Butane trail. When the last rider disappeared through the gap and was lost in the dust-pall Sal Dormer re-emerged and headed for the line of low hills where Des waited. He stood up, collected his palomino, climbed into the saddle and rode down to meet her.

Even though the girl had spent a sleepless night she still managed to look as fresh as morning dew, and Des Willard's heart seemed to skip a beat as he unwittingly studied her lissom form. She pulled up her mount and smiled at him in a calm, matter-of-fact manner. Des nodded towards the dust-cloud that still hung in the sky.

'That was your pa. It looks like he's heading the horse herd west. Maybe you'd better return now so that you won't detain him any.' Sal Dormer shook her head and her smile widened.

'Maybe the herd's heading west,' she replied. 'I'm certain of one thing though, my father won't be leaving Butane until things have been sorted out. He's a mighty curious man and could no more turn his back on a problem than fly.'

'I didn't think there was a problem.' Des sounded bitter. 'I reckoned everyone thought I was responsible for all that's happened an' so I figured your father would be happy to leave me to the County lawman.'

'He's a mighty good judge of character and I doubt very much his opinion has changed at all since he first decided to help you.' Sal's voice was sharp. 'Anyway, what my father does is up to him. I'm here to help you look after the wounded man. I guess we should get moving so that I can do just that.'

The little sparkle of fire in the girl's big brown eyes restored his humour and, when his face split in a big grin, the laughter lines crinkled around his eyes. 'Yeah. You're plumb right. I guess I'm looking too close at my troubles. I – I'm sure glad you came.' Des turned his palomino as he spoke and urged the animal into a canter. Sal stared at his sturdy frame for a few moments, liking every clear-cut line, then with a softened smile on her face, she sent her mount to follow the smooth-running palomino.

By the time they arrived at the canyon where Squinty Robins held on to life by the merest thread, Des had recounted all that had happened to him since the first time he had called at the banker's home the previous night. The way he told her of Ike Somers' death convinced her that he had never previously killed anyone and she knew that, although he might have cause to kill again and again, he would never do so wantonly. He was not, and never would be, a man to glory in gunplay for its own sake.

When they knelt each side of Squinty the doubts crowded in. His pallid cheeks held the look of death, and it was a long time before they decided the pulse movement was positive and not just the throbbing of blood in their own fingers. Sal had brought plenty of dressings and when Des boiled up a dixie of water she set to cleaning and sterilising the wound. Then with an expertise that Des admired she dressed the wound and bound the dressing in place. She had also brought a number of cans containing clear soup and, when she warmed one up to a suitable temperature, she cradled Squinty's head in her lap while she fed it to him in the minutest trickles.

An hour or so later they sat together and ate a breakfast of pork, beans and hunks of pemmican. They sat quite close, each eager for the physical contact with the other, and when their hands met as they passed food to each other and refilled mugs with coffee, the sensation stirred them deeply. When Des gave her his arm to help her to her feet after the meal she came up as light as a feather. She held on to his arm just that fraction longer and her nearness edged away any restraint he might have felt.

With a gasp he pulled her close and for a long time looked down into the depths of her brown eyes as her lean, young body pressed unashamedly into him. Her eyes closed and her shapely lips parted in an open invitation. The kiss lasted a long time and opened up vistas of happiness for each of them. They both knew with certainty that they belonged to each other for all time. The hot blood flowing in young veins made itself felt but although Sal made no attempt to ease herself away from him he knew that he had reached the limit of her surrender until they were legally joined.

They came apart and he held her at arm's length, his breathing fast, and excitement gleaming in his blue eyes. There was tenderness in Sal's face but no smile as her eyes opened. Loving each other was one thing, but being free to love each other was another and the thought had crowded in upon her that her man was hunted.

'God, Sal! I love you,' he breathed, and she nodded gravely.

'I know – I know,' she repeated. 'It's just as well, I guess, because I'm aiming to spend the rest of my life with you.'

Des made to pull her close again but she resisted and stood away from him.

'For things to come out right for us we've got to get Robins back to talking,' she said quietly. 'Let's concentrate on that.'

Des nodded his agreement and fought down the impulses that crowded in. Selecting another can of tinned soup he set about heating it. The girl's eyes watching him were velvet-soft. Her colour mounted as the thought fleeted through her mind that she would gladly dispense with the legal rigmarole if he were to remain outside the law. Des, wholly absorbed in his task, knew nothing of her thoughts and, when he ultimately joined her with the soup, Sal was cool and controlled.

Just a mile or so north of Butane, Seth Dormer and Jack Mallory parted company with the herd. Abe Cotton's blistering remarks cut clean through Mallory's tiredness and depression when Dormer stated he was staying on a while in Butane, but Dormer was unmoved. He affected not to hear the vitriolic outpouring of his scout and sat wooden-faced while the entire herd streamed past. The two men watched until the drag riders were lost in the dust, then they edged their mounts on to the trail and made for town.

There was an indefinable quality in the air that told them things had happened since they were last in town, an urgency about the way men moved along the sidewalks and the animation among the small groups who sheltered here and there in the shade of buildings from the scorching sun.

Slim Manning stood with a dozen or so townsfolk just outside the bank and Ed Slade the teller was in the doorway, a pile of ledgers under his arm. There was a serious look on his face and his words seemed to have a sobering effect on the listeners. Mallory reined in and Dormer stopped his mount just behind.

'I guess Ezra thought the risk worth while,' Ed Slade was saying, and Mallory craned forward in the saddle to hear the better. 'What was this about Ezra Scott?' he thought.

'I guess he gambled for high stakes with his own ante but he's left enough in safe investment to pay back every red cent to all his customers. I reckon Willard took all the ready cash he held here.' As he spoke, Ed Slade stared meaningfully towards the newcomers, and Slim Manning turned, then leaning over the sidewalk rail, his brooding eyes rested on the alkali-covered men.

'That sidekick of yours sure had himself a good time last night,' Manning drawled, his glance now fully directed at Mallory. 'He got clean away with a gold consignment and murdered Ezra Scott for good measure.' Mallory's shocked expression brought a hard smile to the lawman's lips. 'Doc Colehan pulled a .38 slug outa Scott an' Miss Sheila said how Willard called at the house some time earlier on and was told how Ezra was at the bank getting the consignment ready.'

Mallory passed a weary hand over his dust-coated face. This was the last straw. Not for one moment did he question the veracity of Manning's statement. Everything pointed to Des Willard being an out-and-out killer and this was just one more crime to be added to the list. His thoughts turned to Sheila Scott and his sorrow for the girl was deep. To lose her father was bad enough but for it to be at the hands of the man she loved was too much a burden for her to bear. He turned in the saddle to announce his intentions to Seth Dormer, then he rode off towards the Scotts' house.

Dormer stayed on long enough to pose a question to Ed Slade. 'You saying the bank's near broke, mister?'

Manning and the other men glanced in a surprised way at Dormer but Slade's expression was bland.

'If the customers want to draw their money out, then the bank'll be left with next to nothing. Ezra picked some mighty bad investments lately. Maybe if he'd lived he'd have picked himself off the floor again but he didn't get the chance, I guess. These tell the story.' He tapped the ledgers significantly.

'You got any objection to me taking a look?'

Ed Slade shrugged his shoulders but there was a light in his eyes that Dormer recognised. He knew a killer when he saw one. 'I don't know that it's any business of yours mister,' Slade said calmly. 'Not being a customer or a citizen of Butane, but, for my part, you're welcome to take a look-see.'

If Slade expected Dormer to be satisfied by his reply he was doomed to disappointment. Dormer slid out of the saddle and, tying his mount to the hitchrail, stepped up to the sidewalk. He brushed past Manning and, ignoring the other men, headed Slade inside. Ed Slade kept himself under rigid control and by the time he had the ledgers open on the long counter he looked every inch the bank-teller.

Dormer built himself a cigarette before addressing himself to the neatly written ledger entries. He knew after scanning a few pages that no errors would show up, the entries had been made by a craftsman and the story unfolded would undoubtedly tie up with Ed Slade's statement. 'You're a careful worker, Slade,' he murmured and a glint of wicked humour appeared in the teller's eyes to disappear as quickly at Dormer's next remark. 'Now, if I'd been handling these ledgers through the years, they'd have gathered some dirt here and there.'

Ed Slade merely shrugged but there was an air of watchfulness about him. Dormer switched his attention to the final figures. Investments matched the balance to within a few hundred dollars. 'So Ezra Scott's daughter gets nothing,' he remarked. Slade nodded.

'Yeah, she's plumb unlucky that Ezra died when he did. There was always the chance he'd have taken up some good investments if he'd lived.'

'Up to a couple of years ago he'd kept his investments in line with the Chase National, how come he turned lone wolf?'

For a brief instant Slade allowed a look of mingled respect and hate to show on his face. 'I guess he got greedy. He kept his reasons mighty close, though, and it could be he got fed some bad information. Anyway, mister, all I had to do was keep the books, he never asked for my say-so.'

'And what are you going to do now if the bank folds up?'

Ed Slade's eyes became ice-cold and when he spoke Dormer felt the evil strength of the man. 'Maybe I'll start a bank, mister. I've been mighty careful with my dinero and I'm not likely to make the same mistakes as Ezra Scott.'

Seth Dormer grinned but without humour. 'Y'know,' he said. 'I had a kinda hunch you'd say just that.' He turned abruptly on his heels and moved out of the bank to the sidewalk. Then, leaving his mount tethered to the hitchrail, he made his way to Sheila Scott's house.

Jack Mallory waited with mixed feelings at the Scotts' house after having rapped his knuckles on the solid front door. He tried to analyse his feelings but found difficulty in thinking straight. One thing was for sure, he loved Sheila the way he would love no one else and felt physical pain at the thought of the torment besetting her. His long-term chances of claiming her now were good but the cost was too great for contemplation. His lifelong friend had had to turn killer and she had perforce to lose her father before the way was clear for him; it was a sorry path to tread for his reward.

So troubled was he that the door opened without him noticing. There was a moment when he looked in the deep blue eyes that had spent themselves of tears, then she was in his arms, holding on tight, gaining comfort from his strength. He lifted her through the doorway and closed the door behind them.

'Oh, Jack,' she murmured. 'You've heard what's happened?'

The shyness he had felt with her over the years since she had blossomed into womanhood dropped away and he held her tightly to him as he replied, 'Yes. I know about your pa and I'm sure sorry. If there's anything that needs attending to, then I want to help.'

She eased herself away a little and he

dropped his arms, allowing her to lead the way into the living-room. Sheila poured him a drink then stood a couple of paces away from him beside the vast open fireplace. 'I guess I counted on you helping me,' she said quietly, her solemn glance resting on his alkali-covered face. The thought flashed through his mind that she had found him dependable enough but wanting in what it took to be her mate. He marvelled that Des Willard could treat her love with such scant regard. To turn his back on her was unbelievable, but to kill her father into the bargain was beyond reason.

'It seems it's all my fault, Sheila,' Mallory said. 'If I hadn't persuaded Willard to come back to my place he'd have kept going into the sun. It looks like all I did was bring you grief.' The girl said nothing but her eyes were soft. 'I guess I just couldn't believe he was a killer at that time an' I reckoned that if he could be cleared, then the way would be easy for you both.'

'And that's what you wanted, Jack Mallory?' The soft look had gone from her eyes again but they glistened as moisture sprung into them.

The question took him by surprise and his reply came fast, unthinking. 'Not what I wanted, what I reckoned you wanted.'

'Then you're wrong, Jack Mallory! That's never what I wanted, nor did I want Des

Willard. I wanted to believe he was not a killer but that's as far as it went.' A deep emotion had taken hold of her and she stared at him intensely, her body rigid. 'Why should it be Des Willard I wanted?'

'You were always mighty close. I took it to be that way.' He looked up from studying his boots and gazed into her face frankly. It was then he plumbed the depths of her mind and his whole being surged with the wonder of it. Without knowing how they had come together, he was holding her, conscious of her firm breasts pressing into him and of the passion that consumed him, making her press tighter to him as she matched his ardour. He kissed her and they stayed a long time, savouring each other, their bodies taut, eager. They came apart when the knock came at the door and it took some seconds for them to appreciate the first magic moment was gone.

Chapter Eight

'Where's Sal?' Seth Dormer asked when he entered the room and reached for the drink Sheila had poured for him. He affected not to notice the girl's flushed face when she answered.

'She went riding this morning just after sun-up and it's my belief she's gone to help Des Willard.' Jack Mallory stared at Sheila but Seth Dormer's expression did not change. 'Des Willard came back here last night and I was pretty near to shooting him. Somehow I couldn't bring myself to do that and I left him talking to Sal. She stayed with me until sun-up, then rode out of town.'

'You going to trail her?' Mallory asked Dormer, dragging his eyes away from Sheila. 'Des Willard's no fit company for Sal.'

There was a hint of a smile on Dormer's face when he shook his head. 'Nope. I set a lot of store on Sal's good sense and judgment. If she reckons Willard's deserving of help then I'm willing to bet she's right. Maybe it's because I still think so anyway that I'm not worried. Things are still working out too pat to be true. Your father's been shot, Miss Sheila, and I'm plumb sorry, but it strikes me that other folk have gained a lot more from the killings on this range than Des Willard. Furthermore, if Willard had killed your pa and cleaned up that consignment, he wouldn't be kicking his heels in this territory now. That would have added up to staking himself for a long ride. I gather Ed Slade's told you that the bank can pay its customers and no more.'

Mallory shot a questioning look at Dormer as Sheila nodded.

'Yes. It seems my father made some chancy investments that went wrong.'

Dormer looked pensive, then after lighting a cigarette. 'I'd be obliged if you did some riding for me, Mallory. I've a heap of questions I want telegraphed to the Chase National Bank headquarters in New York, and I guess the telegraph would be best sent from Pecos.'

Mallory was about to ask questions, then thought better of it. 'Sure thing,' he replied. 'Just give me enough time to rest my cayuse and I'll hit the trail.'

'While you're heading for Pecos it's not going to take you far out of your way to catch up with Abe Cotton an' the boys. Tell Abe to find a decent spot to peg down the herd and to hightail it back to town with as many men as can be spared from droving duties.'

'I reckon you know what you're doing,'

Mallory said. 'So I'll do like you say.'

Dormer nodded his thanks. 'Can't say I know what I'm doing, Jack, but I've got a feeling that things can be brought to the boil in Butane mighty soon. It's just a hunch but I've felt the same at other times and I've been right.'

'I can't see what there is to bring to the boil, excepting stirring up a posse to bring Willard in to answer for his crimes.'

'It figures you'd be bitter, considering you and Willard have been pards a long time and the way things have been made to add up. It could be though we've been doing the wrong sums.' Dormer smiled slyly as he spoke, but he did not elaborate, instead he turned to Sheila, his face full of compassion. 'I'll move into the hotel now, ma'am and I'll be looking in to see you from time to time, anything that wants doing leave to me. Just one thing, don't sign anything that anyone might bring to you and don't give permission for Slade to pay out any of the bank's customers, at least no more on demand than a normal request.'

'I'll do just as you say, Mr Dormer – and thanks,' Sheila replied. She was more composed now. The terrible loss she had sustained had been tempered by the sure knowledge she had won her man, and with the competent, cool Seth Dormer to lean upon as well, her future had brightened considerably within the hour. When Dormer turned to go, Mallory made to go with him, then impulsively he turned, took the girl in his arms and kissed her without passion, but possessively.

'Take care.' She whispered the words as he let her go and his smile reassured her.

Mallory got to the door as the staccato report of a rifle cracked through the stifling stillness of the air. He saw Seth Dormer pitch forward into the dirt path and out of the corner of his eye saw the sun glint on the rifle barrel as it disappeared through the open window of the upper floor of the Maverick. He hurried to Dormer's side and laughed his relief when the horse-dealer hauled himself up on to his knees. There was a livid weal across Dormer's neck just below the ear but even though the blood gathered on the wound quickly, Mallory could see it was nothing serious. Sheila was beside him when he helped Dormer to his feet.

'That was mighty close.' Seth Dormer moved his head to and fro tentatively as he spoke and winced a little with the pain of it. 'Things sure are starting to boil. It seems folk don't like the sort of questions I've been asking.'

The horse-dealer allowed himself to be piloted back into the house by the girl, who was eager to dress the wound, but Mallory, instead of following, made his way swiftly along the sidewalk to the Maverick. The sudden stir of excitement the shot had caused had died as quickly. No one had seen Dormer fall, so in a matter of seconds the shot was forgotten and the few people he passed gave him no more than an incurious glance.

Ignoring the saloon entrance he entered the hotel section and, as he mounted the stairs, three men abreast turned the corner just above him. They were Dainton's right-hand men, Tyler, Creasey and Nolan. They paused and eyed him without interest as he stopped and stared up at them. A shadow crossed Mallory's path as someone else entered the vestibule and he glanced round to find Slim Manning's bitter eyes upon him.

'Which one of you hombres took a shot at Seth Dormer?' Mallory asked quietly.

Nolan glanced first at Tyler and then at Creasey, an exaggerated look of surprise on his face. 'You hear what Mallory asked? You fellers been throwing promiscuous lead?'

Tyler and Creasey shook their heads. 'Nope we ain't,' Tyler's gravelly voice grated. 'You aint neither 'cos we've been together since we hit town.'

'You're lying.' Mallory's voice did not rise any but it was ice-cold. 'One of you hombres used a rifle from up there just a couple of minutes ago. Let's take a look-see for the rifle.'

'You take a look, Mallory. I'm taking a drink to clear the alkali outa my throat.' Nolan's big, dark face was bereft of humour now. 'So just step outa my way.'

Mallory stepped back down the stairs and stepped aside so that Slim Manning was also in his sight. He had no faith in Manning as a lawman. A sneering smile crossed Nolan's face as he started down the stairs but vanished when Mallory's guns appeared with silk-smooth speed. One gun covered Manning and Mallory motioned him on in. 'Come right on in, Manning, you're the lawman, join us and we'll look for the rifle.'

'You gone loco, Mallory?' Manning rasped.

'Stow the talk, just unbuckle your gunbelts – that goes for you too, Manning – and let 'em drop.'

For a long minute the four men glared at Mallory, debating whether to ignore the instructions, but there was a set to the horse-rancher's features that told them he was in deadly earnest, and first Manning then the other three unbuckled their gunbelts and let them crash on to the stairs.

'Right. Up you go and remember, any clever stuff and you, Manning, get ventilated.'

The four men stomped up the stairs ahead of Mallory but they did not appear unduly concerned. At the head of the stairs they waited for Mallory's instructions. He nodded towards the doors that led into rooms over-looking Main Street, and Manning opened up one after another. There were yells of indignation from two where some floor-show women were dressing for the day, from another one a lazy invitation rang out from a woman sitting on the edge of the bed, completely nude, contemplating an array of frilly dresses draped over chairs. In the fourth room, the one that Mallory judged was the place from where the gunman had fired the shot, Kay Lane the risque, dance-routine expert was still in bed. The way she looked she needed a lot more time there before she would be fresh enough for the day's work.

Mallory's eyes swept around the room, then ignoring the sleepy-eyed dancer, crossed to the clothes cupboard and poked around inside. He had no luck. His glance took in the space under the bed, the coverlets did not quite reach to the floor, but no rifle nestled on the floorboards. Then he crossed to the window and looked out across to the Scotts' house, the angle was just right, the shot had come from this room. He failed to see Kay Lane's eye wink its message to Nolan, whose face wore an evil smile of triumph.

'Hey – Jack Mallory. If you're set on joining me get rid of those apes first. A crowd's all right for a dance routine but what goes on in a bedroom's sorta private.'

Mallory's colour deepened as he looked

144

into Kay Lane's mocking eyes and the hoarse laughter from the men at the door did not help him much either. He knew he would get small change out of Kay Lane by questioning and there was nothing left for him to do but back down. There was no doubt that somewhere in the Maverick hotel the rifle was reposing, but they had been too smart for him. He motioned the four grinning men aside and, keeping his guns trained on them, eased past to the corridor. He was about to head for the stairs when Manning spoke.

'Mallory! When you've got something to investigate the next time, use the law. You try getting the drop on me again and I'll see just how good you are with those smoke-poles. There was a shot right enough and I was investigating, that's my job. I'd rather not have your help.'

'When someone tries ambushing any friend of mine I'll make my own investigations,' Mallory replied. 'I reckon I stand more chance of coming up with the right answers.' Turning on his heels he hurried down the stairs and out into the street. Manning followed him more slowly, the other three stayed inside the doorway of Kay Lane's bedroom.

The dancer eased her body up carefully and, sitting up, hauled the rifle she had been lying on out of the bed. Nolan crossed to her and, taking the rifle, placed it in the clothes cupboard.

'I'm mighty obliged, Kay,' he grunted. 'I reckoned he'd have found the evidence – not that it would have done him any good.'

'I wouldn't have done it for many other men,' the dancer replied. 'A rifle is sure poor company in bed. It's brought up bruises in places it ain't lady-like to mention.'

Nolan tossed a couple of bills on to the bed with a grin. 'I'll take a look-see at them bruises tonight after the floor-show.'

'Yeah I'd like that, but beat it now, I want to catch up with my sleep.'

Nolan nodded and ushered the other two grinning men out of the room. 'Guess I must have made a bad job of it,' he grumbled. 'Mallory didn't say Dormer was dead. Dainton's gonna be a mite upset, but what in Hades he wants Dormer eliminated for beats me. It looked like he was heading outa the territory.'

'It was after he saw Ed Slade the idea came to him,' Tyler put in. 'I'm getting to thinking a lot of Dainton's ideas get born when he's with Slade.'

Nolan paused in the act of picking his gunbelt up off the stairs and fixed Tyler with his glittering eyes. 'There's no call for you to get thinking at all,' he snarled. 'You get paid a durned sight more'n top-hand pay for doing what you're told. Leave all the thinking to Dainton, that way you'll end up with

146

all the dinero you can handle. You think too much an' get around to talking an' maybe you'll end up with a load of lead in your innards.'

'Aw keep your hair on, Mike,' Tyler grumbled. 'It ain't nothing to me anyways.'

'Maybe it is to me, though,' Creasey intervened.

Nolan's eyes lost the glitter when he turned to the second man. Tyler could be brow-beaten but Creasey was of a different calibre. Nolan had never been sure of his ability to outfight Creasey. There was an inherent laziness in the man that permitted him to extend himself at any time only so far as the occasion demanded. 'How come?' Nolan spoke softly as they stepped down to the vestibule.

Creasey looked into the reception-box before replying. 'Always somebody wants somebody else to do the dirty work, and the hombre doing the chore always gets a smaller pay-off.' He paused. 'You know why that is?' Nolan shook his head. 'Because the hombre doing the chore don't know enough about the feller he's working for. If Dainton's the big boss, then that's fine, we know plenty, but if he's taking orders, then I want to know whose orders.'

Nolan digested this for some time and the logic percolated through his thick skull, but his rating for Slade was not too high. 'The

147

way Hubert tells it is they knew each other some place else a long time ago an' Slade gets a bit loose-mouthed when they drink together, that's how we've heard about the shipments we've muscled in on. I reckon that's the way it is.'

Creasey shrugged his shoulders. 'I guess it sounds like sense,' he replied. He was by no means convinced but he reckoned he could wait until something turned up to convince him. 'There's no sense in palavering anyhow, my throat's that choked with alkali it's hard work.' His words appealed to the others' crying needs and they pushed their way into the Maverick saloon section.

When Mallory called back to the Scotts' house, Dormer was sitting on the big leather settle, holding a full glass of rye, his neck was neatly bandaged and he looked at peace with the world. Sheila's eyes brightened at the sight of the younger man and, without first asking, brought him a drink.

'You didn't find out who fired the shot?' Dormer stated more than asked.

'Oh, I know who fired it right enough, but I couldn't find the evidence.' He went on to tell them what had happened. Sheila's face went red and she looked a bit indignant when he recounted looking into the dance-hostesses rooms. Dormer's face split into a wide grin.

'I guess you're too much of a gentleman,

148

Jack,' Dormer said. 'Now me. I'd have found that rifle first time.'

'How so?'

'Right in that Kay Lane's bed, I should say.'

'You reckon so?' Mallory stood up and he saw the colour deepen on Sheila's face. 'I'll go an' check on it.'

'You dare, Jack Mallory!– You dare! and – and.' She saw his grin and her voice tailed away.

He shook his head. 'No need – just knowing who is good enough,' and Seth Dormer nodded agreement.

'Now before you get on your way, Jack, is there any place you know where Willard might have holed up? Some place you knew as youngsters. I know that in the Black Hill country where I was raised there were a couple of places tucked away in the foothills that no one set foot in except my pard and me.'

Mallory thought a moment. It had been a long time now since he had ridden the boyhood trails, then he nodded. 'I guess he could be holed up in one of two places and they both lead off his range.' He searched in his pocket and dug out a piece of pencil, and, divining his next need, Sheila went to a mahogany bureau and brought him a piece of paper.

Carefully Mallory drew in all the features

149

he could remember leading from Butane to the two hidden canyons. Dormer watched him closely and even though he had only ridden along that stretch once in daylight his keen memory brought the entire picture back. 'It's my bet Des would choose this one.' Mallory pointed to the nearest canyon to Butane. 'The water's brought a lot of soil down with it through the years and in places there's mighty good graze, plenty of cover too.'

Dormer picked up the piece of paper and tore it into bits. 'I'll rest up a bit, then I guess I'll take a look at those canyons. Just tell Abe Cotton to keep the boys toned up for action if I'm not here when they hit town.'

'Sure thing, and look out for those hombres who tried their hand at ventilating you.' Mallory reached over and held Sheila's hand briefly, then hurried out.

'You'll stay here, Mr Dormer?' Sheila asked. 'It'll be safer here than in the hotel.' She paused. 'I – I'll feel happier with you around too.'

He smiled and she noticed how white and even his teeth were. 'It certainly does me good to hear my company gives you pleasure. Sure I'll stay and I'm obliged.' He knew that at this time the busier Sheila could be made the better, somebody to look after would take her mind off her father's death and her concern for Jack Mallory's safety.

150

His smile widened as she went into the kitchen to prepare a meal for him, the spring was back in her step. His smile faded a bit as his thoughts turned to his daughter Sal. She would need a lot of luck before her future ironed itself out. His modesty would never have permitted him to say nor even think it, but had Sal been asked, she would have said she could do without luck so long as her father was rooting for her. He would take this range apart to allow his daughter to have a future so long as he was convinced that Des Willard was not a murderer. His reason told him that Willard was being framed, and his own judgment of character confirmed his reasoning. The next meeting would decide his course of action he thought, then, characteristically, gave up the problem until the time came for dealing with it.

'Nobody's showed up yet toting Squinty,' Ed Slade murmured to Hubert Dainton.

They were sitting in a quiet corner of the Maverick saloon, sharing a bottle of bourbon. Ed Slade had closed the bank for a day as a mark of respect to Ezra Scott and with as sorrowful a mien as possible he tried to drink away his grief. At least that's the way it looked to the folk of Butane.

'Mebbe that bronc of his took him back to Box Q range, if so, it'll take some time for him to be noticed – a lot more men died there last night.' Dainton spoke with a show of enthusiasm. 'Most of Somers' men went to Boot Hill an' Genner with the rest of the old Box Q hands. We caught 'em stealing stock an' fighting one another. It was easy for us, especially because we had the backing of Dormer's men and Mallory.' Dainton reached for another drink and laughed as he recalled the night's work. 'It sure is something when you get your enemies fighting your battles.'

Slim Manning came into the saloon from the street entrance and, after nodding to Dainton, stood up to the bar and called for a drink. Dainton crossed over to him.

'I heard a shot a few minutes ago,' he said. 'Anybody get hurt?'

Slim Manning gave him a long look. 'Nope – not that I know. I guess Nolan missed.'

It was Dainton's turn to stare. 'Nolan?'

'Yeah. Leastwise that's what Jack Mallory says. He took me and your three sidekicks on a tour of the rooms upstairs on the end of his guns to look for the evidence.'

Dainton laughed softly. 'He sure is a hellraiser that Mallory,' he said. 'He's a mite foolish though, bucking the law with a gun, he kinda gives you the excuse to ventilate him next time you meet up.'

'I might do just that.' Manning replied, and Dainton returned to his table, well satisfied. Another chance would come to get Dormer,

152

and Mallory should now be taken care of. He passed the information to Slade more in the manner of a man discussing the price of horseflesh, and Slade muttered his advice.

'It'll take a long time for Manning to rake up the gall to take Mallory. I'd put Nolan on to trailing Dormer and Creasey on to Mallory. Those two jaspers are smart enough to finish the job. If Dormer and Mallory stay close, then let Tyler join up with the other two; it's my opinion Tyler works better when he's got company.'

The three men in question came into the bar at that moment from the adjoining door to the hotel section. They gave their boss a look that would have told him they had fallen down on their chore, and walked on up to the bar. When Slade left, they joined Dainton at the table.

Chapter Nine

It needed a couple of hours to sundown when Seth Dormer rode out of Butane. He left a town alive with the excitement of forming a posse to hunt down Des Willard. The killing of Ezra Scott had acted upon the townsfolk like a festering sore, until they had reached the point where it was not enough that Willard would be apprehended some day, some place else. They wanted to see him hanging right there, on the tall juniper tree that stood like a lone sentinel behind the jailhouse. He had noticed that Slim Manning was being pushed into heading the posse. The Deputy was not wildly enthusiastic, and Dormer noticed too that Dainton and his men held themselves aloof from the lusting crowd. Hank Kershawe, the stage-owner, and Dan Smeaton, the Indian trader, did most of the shouting because that was the way they were built.

He took the southern trail just ten minutes after the Alpine stage left the depot, timing it deliberately in the event of being followed. He reckoned he would reach the cover of the stagecoach dust just when he wanted to slip off the trail through the cut in Alpine Bluff

154

that would lead him back through the mountain on to the open range. By the time he followed the stage through Alpine Bluff canyon he had no positive sight of a rider but his instinct told him he was being tagged. Turning at length through the cut, he rode his horse up and down the stream at the other end before setting off for a pair of hills due east, leaving a trail that a tenderfoot could follow.

With the sun about to tip behind the Silver Mountains, Dormer saw the horse and rider emerge out of the gap and work up and down the stream until picking up the trail. Even at the distance he recognised Nolan. When night fell, the horse-herder had obliterated his trail and had worked around the hill to play his deadly game of tag.

The night sped away with Nolan using his skill and nerve in his will-o'-the-wisp search, and with goose-pimples standing out on his skin as doubts crowded in. With the first light of dawn he was about to skirt a dry-wash when Dormer's voice cut shrill across the music of the cicades.

'Stop, Nolan!'

Nolan did as he was told and Dormer edged the roan out from the cover of a vast rock. 'Well, you've found me, Nolan. Now what?'

'I've got better things to do than look for you, Dormer, so stop playing games.'

'No dice, Nolan.' Dormer's voice was ice-cold. 'I've had you in my sights from the time we left town. You should have kept on going behind that stage to Alpine, back-tracking sure gave your intentions away.'

'If you'd kept tabs on me, Dormer, you'd have seen me catch that stage and hand the driver a package for Alpine, an' right now I'm heading for Dainton's range.'

'Well, that being so I'm sure sorry for you, because you're going to die anyhow.'

Nolan stiffened in the saddle, and the fleeting thought of Dainton and Slade sharing a bottle of bourbon in Maverick made him want to scream his resentment at putting his life on the line. Dormer's words gave him no comfort.

'You just take your time, Nolan. I'm going to count to five an' then I'm shooting you whether you draw or not. One-Two-Three.'

Fear made Nolan make his move but in no sense did it affect his speed. Against most men his skill would have sufficed, but that was no satisfaction to him as he pitched out of the saddle with a neat hole drilled through his forehead.

Seth Dormer hefted Nolan's body across the saddle of the dead man's horse and, tying the animal's lead rein to his own saddle cantle, headed north-west until just two miles short of Butane, then, untying the lead rein, he sent the animal scampering home with a sharp slap to the rump.

A couple of hours riding brought Dormer to the line-shack that still housed the mortal remains of Ike Somers. He gave it a wide berth. The shack served the purpose of fixing his position in relation to the blind canyon, so he rode on, his sharp eyes searching the steep-sided mountain for the narrow entry. When he found the split in the rock-face he understood why folks passed it by without a second glance. There was barely width for a horse to pass and the overhang seemed ready to fall at any moment and so block the entry. A rider would hesitate to take his mount into such a confined space and as Dormer coaxed his roan deeper into the mountain, with the passage remaining the same width, he could picture men having got so far on foot then retracing their steps convinced the split led nowhere. He was beginning to have qualms when the passage swung in a wide arc then widened, and he found his horse walking on grass.

'Keep coming!' The peremptory order came from the black mass of a boulder just ahead of him and Seth Dormer obliged.

'Hold it right there!' Dormer did as he was told. He recognised Des Willard's voice and, considering Willard had his daughter tucked away up in this canyon, he was pleased that the young man was so much on the *qui vive*.

There was a brief pause while Des moved

around the boulder, then he emerged on to the trail. 'Mr Dormer! How in Hades did you find this place?'

Dormer slid out of the saddle and busied himself with making a smoke. 'Mallory spelled out a couple of likely places for me,' he replied quietly. 'I guess I'm lucky to have picked the right place first.'

'Well, I'm sure glad to see you,' Des replied, coming close to the older man and taking the proffered tobacco sac.

'What makes you so glad? Maybe I'm here on account I'm a US Marshal and you're wanted in town.'

'It could be, but I reckon not,' Des replied. 'You're here on account of Sal and the way you came tells me that you're not considering taking me in. You'd have ghosted your way in if you were set on that chore.'

Dormer laughed and drew deep on his cigarette before replying. 'Yeah, I'd have been a mite more careful. Well, let's get to your hideout, I'd sure give something for a man-sized mug of coffee.'

Des Willard led the way and Dormer followed on foot, leading his roan by the lead rein. They hugged the left-hand wall of the canyon that veered away in a long arc, until at length they arrived at the snug shelter set deep under an overhang, where a fire burned brightly, lighting up the still form of Squinty Robins and Sal Dormer's alert face as she looked up from where she had sat with her head bowed in sleep. For a brief moment the fire showed up the alarm in the girl's eyes as she realised two people were approaching, then her face radiated a smile of welcome as she recognised them. She stood up and came to meet them.

'I'm glad you've come,' she said simply, taking her father's big hand into her own. 'Now you can help.'

Dormer gripped her hand but said nothing. They moved back to the fireside and he took a long look at Squinty Robins before taking a seat beside his daughter. 'What happened to him?' he asked, nodding towards the Box Q cook.

Des Willard looked up from the pot of coffee he had placed over the fire. 'That's what we're hoping to find out. I found him a few miles out of town an' this is what I dug out of him.' Des searched inside his vest pocket and handed across the partially flattened slug he had taken out of Squinty.

Dormer took it and held it to the firelight. 'Mm, a .38.'

'Yeah.' Willard's tone was dry. 'So someone else in town, with a yen for killing is using .38 slugs. It naturally follows to me that the same hombre killed Suter and Ezra Scott, and if only we can get Squinty well enough to say his piece, then I get cleared and we clean up the territory.'

'And how're you making out with him? D'you think he'll get around to talking?'

'He'll talk sooner than you think,' Sal chipped in. 'He's swallowing nourishment now and you can feel his pulse going. So long as the wound is kept clean, there's no reason why he shouldn't mend.'

A big smile crossed Willard's features and, Seth Dormer, watching him, appreciated the attraction the younger man held for women. The smile lit his handsome face like a beacon and his teeth gleamed in the firelight, white and even.

'I'm sure glad to hear you say that, Sal; I've been thinking he'd gone too far.' The measure of relief in Des Willard's voice was enough to convince Seth Dormer of the man's absolute innocence of the killings Willard had allegedly committed, and any qualms he might have felt concerning his daughter's feelings for Willard melted away. She could do a lot worse for herself, he reckoned.

Dormer stood up and crossed again to where Squinty lay. He felt the man's pulse and watched a little nerve move rhythmically on the side of the face, the eyeballs seemed to be moving a little under the lids too. There was no doubt in his mind that about midday Squinty would be taking notice. 'I guess Sal is right,' he remarked as he resumed his place by the fire. 'It's gonna be a long time before he gets around to earning his keep again but I'm thinking we can get him back to town on a travois to say his piece. Once he comes out of that coma he'll fight good and hard to get better. These small stringy hombres are all the same – they take a whole lot of punishment.'

Des Willard poured three mugs of coffee from the bubbling pot and handed one each to Sal and her father. He took a tentative sip from his own mug, then set it down close to the fire. 'I'll go and unsaddle your cayuse,' he said and he left father and daughter together.

Seth Dormer smoked in silence for a few minutes, then he turned to look into Sal's face. 'How much does it matter to you Sal whether young Willard's a killer or not?' he asked quietly.

She did not answer for a long time and he could see her fighting back the quick answer and composing her expression. When she spoke it was quietly and matter-of-factly. 'I guess it means about everything to me.'

He reached over and grasped her hand reassuringly.

'I've got no doubts,' she continued. 'How about you?'

Seth Dormer smiled and shook his head. 'No – I guess we'll just have to get things sorted out then get you hitched up before taking the herd east.' He paused, 'That's if you aim to get wed.'

Sal laughed and pressed his hand warmly. 'That's just what I aim to do.'

'Well, just get him to ask my permission first. I'd sure hate him to think my daughter wears the pants in my family.'

When Des returned and sat down with his mug of coffee, Dormer decided to outline the best course of action. 'I guess you might as well know that when I left town Manning was organising a mighty big posse to hunt you down. There was a lot of talk going on but I reckon they'd have a night's hard drinking under their belts before they hit the trail.'

'They won't get much luck,' Des replied easily. 'Nobody's going to find their way in here.'

'No, I agree, but if the range is going to be swarming with men it could be a bit tricky getting Robins into town unnoticed.' Dormer's expression was serious. 'Now, with the range cleared, we could get Robins into town and safe in the Scott's house ready to say his piece.'

'And how do you propose to clear the range?'

Dormer laughed. 'I don't, that looks like your job. You give 'em sight of yourself and they'll be on your trail to a man.'

'No!' Sal almost shouted the word. 'The risk is too great; they'd ride him down for sure.'

Des shot a grateful look at the indignant girl, he was glad of her concern but totally unmoved regarding his chances of keeping ahead of a posse. It was purely a question of how long he would have to keep in front and on the run.

Dormer went on to clarify this. 'If Robins comes to and shows that he's going to talk, and be able to travel, then give it until a couple of hours before sundown before moving out to let them get a sight of you. Let it look like you're aiming for some place east, then after sundown, cut back through the hills on to the Pecos trail. By my reckoning you should meet up with Mallory round about sun-up. He's on his way back from Pecos and should be bringing some useful information. Your entry into Butane will be backed by a mighty strong crew of my men, I'll send 'em the moment we hit town.'

Sal Dormer looked long and hard at both men and a couple of times framed the words of caution that came uppermost in her mind, but she held her peace. Her father was usually right when it came to planning and it was pretty evident that Des had decided to go along with him. She was wise enough to show no semblance of disagreement when her man was busy committing himself to a course of action. Instead she poured fresh mugs of coffee for the two men, who now sat smoking contentedly. Then, resuming her seat, she rested her head forward into her arms and dozed off to sleep.

Creasey shifted his wad of tobacco from one side of his mouth to the other and scanned the trail that fanned out below him in two directions. His horse stood ground-hitched in a grassy fold farther up the hillside. His features radiated contentment as the rising sun brought the canyons out of the receding gloom. Any time now Mallory would be re-passing this point. He had dogged Mallory all the way from Butane, cold and unremitting as an eagle. When Mallory met up with Dormer's horse-herders Creasey felt keen disappointment, but his spirits had lifted when Mallory left Abe Cotton's crew and pressed on the trail that meant Pecos.

Creasey had made his mind up and headed without hesitation to a spot he knew well. His lips had curled with disgust as he had remembered the last time he had lain waiting in the very place some years ago. He had killed the guard and driver of the Pecos Stage and had discovered an empty Wells Fargo bag with the seals shot off. When Sam and Charlie Lee were caught by Sheriff Suter he had watched them dangle for his crime after they had protested to the last they had robbed the stage barely eight miles out of Pecos. The memory had brought no remorse with it, merely chagrin at his loss.

The man's inherent laziness saved Mallory's life. Having stowed a couple of bottles of bourbon and plenty of hard-tack Creasey had decided to laze away his time and spoil himself until Mallory's return, in preference to rushing the chore and hurrying back to be given further dirty work to do.

For the best part of two full days and nights Creasey had holed up under cover from the searing sun and now, a grin of unholy delight split his lips, as a horse and rider emerged out of the Pecos canyon, and even though a film of dust enveloped them, he recognised the set of Mallory's figure.

Creasey eased his rifle into position, taking great care not to allow the sunlight to glint on the barrel, and slowly, deliberately, brought the advancing Mallory into his sights. The perspiration ran down his forehead but he ignored it as he waited for the range to come right. Already he had picked the spot and inexorably the unsuspecting Mallory drew nearer. Creasey licked his lips in wolfish anticipation and his whole being tingled with the excitement of the kill, then his concentration focused completely. He took in a breath, held it and his trigger finger took the first pressure, then the rock behind which he sheltered seemed to explode as a shell screamed into it and ricocheted madly. His aim went adrift and he slewed around wild-eyed and suddenly afraid.

Chapter Ten

The load was lifted from Des Willard's shoulders. A remarkable change had come over Squinty Robins during the day and he had talked enough to convince his listeners that the way was clear to square the charges laid against Willard. As he coaxed his palomino through the narrow defile towards the plain, Des thrust the lingering pleasurable thoughts of Sal Dormer away from him. From now until the time when his name was cleared, he needed to devote his unrelaxing attention to things of the present. Introspection or reminiscing were indulgences he could not afford. Now he knew the ante and now he was convinced of his right to keep himself alive at all costs.

There was a basic difference in his attitude towards his problems now. With the near certainty of Squinty Robins staying alive to say his piece, Des felt he would be fighting from a position of strength. The law as vested in Seth Dormer was on his side, so any gunplay that was necessary to keep a whole skin would be accepted by the law and he was good and ready to trade lead with anybody who was prepared to stand

166

between him and his right to take back the Box Q.

He pulled the palomino to a stop about twenty yards from the mouth of the narrow fissure and rechecked his six-guns. Then, satisfied, he guided his mount on to the level ground of the plain and came face to face with the two men who had shouted loudest for his scalp.

Dan Smeaton, the Indian trader, and Hank Kershawe, the stage-line owner, were on their way back to town. They had made their token ride with Manning's posse and were now set on getting to the Maverick's long bar just as soon as their rangy-looking cayuses could carry them there. They stared in blank surprise at Des Willard as he seemed to spring out of the very mountain and neither of them liked the set, expressionless face that stared back at them unwinkingly.

'It sure is your lucky day,' Des remarked easily. 'Half of Butane out gunning for me and it had to be you who found me. What's it to be? You taking me in dead or alive?'

Dan Smeaton recovered quickly and grinned a bit uncertainly. 'It don't matter two straws to us, Willard, whether you get taken in or not. Right now we're heading for town and something to clear the alkali outa our throats.'

Willard's face was mocking as Kershawe nodded agreement with his crony's remarks.

167

'I always figured you hombres were nothing but loud-mouths. If you had a few more men between you and me you'd be shouting on them to draw.'

'You've got us figured all wrong, Willard,' Kershawe put in quickly.

'Maybe, but you're going to draw or I'll gun you down. I'm taking no chances on you spreading the news you've seen me. Dead men don't talk and that's the way you're going to be.'

Kershawe swallowed hard and experienced trouble in finding his voice. 'There's no sense in adding two more killings to the list, Willard,' he croaked. 'You just stay there and you'll see us head straight for town.'

'Nope!' Willard was emphatic. 'There's no sense in not adding two more killings to the list,' he pointed out. 'They'll hang me for one just as sure as four, leastways with you hombres dead there'll be two less shouting for my neck.'

There was a throaty laugh from Dan Smeaton and Des shot a quick glance over his right shoulder. A bunch of riders came clear out of the haze about a mile away and immediately changed direction. Time suddenly became short. 'Looks like you've run plumb outa luck, Willard,' Smeaton sneered. 'That's Manning for sure.'

Des shrugged his wide shoulders. He knew there was no time now to taunt the two men into action but he did not allow his need for haste to show through. 'Just unbuckle those gunbelts pronto or I'll drop you for sure.'

Kershawe did what he was told quickly, but the approaching riders egged on Smeaton's vanity. Here was his big chance to walk tall in Butane. Willard must be rattled by the muffled hoofbeats and he, Smeaton, was a match for most men from an even start. The Indian trader's hand came slowly around to the front of his belt and there was a look of resignation on his face, then he kneed his mount into Kershawe's and his hand flashed back for his six-gun.

Smeaton's assessment of Des Willard was wrong but he never had occasion to dwell on the fact. Willard's attention had been focused on Smeaton one hundred per cent and the hole in the man's forehead as he slumped half across his sidekick's horse was grim testimony to Willard's dedication. Kershawe gaped at the smooth speed of Willard's draw and the awful final accuracy. He pushed hard against Smeaton's body, sending it sliding to the ground and gasped his relief as Willard's palomino was galvanised into action and horse and rider moved rapidly out of range.

A couple of the riders detached themselves from the bunch and bore down upon Kershawe, the others, recognising Willard, spurred their mounts after him. Kershawe was rebuckling his gunbelt when Slim Manning and Lew Foster, a gambler on the El Paso and Austin circuit, pulled up and dropped to the ground. Manning turned Smeaton's body over and studied the discoloured wound briefly, his enthusiasm for the chase evaporating. The rest of his men disappeared over the breast of a rise, while Willard was lost in the rolling terrain.

'That hombre is sure enough playing for keeps,' Lew Foster remarked as he lit a cheroot. 'Can't see any future in crowding him, so I guess I'll give Kershawe a hand toting Smeaton into town.' Foster laughed unfeelingly as Manning glared before climbing back into the saddle and riding slowly in the general direction of the posse.

Des Willard was filled with quiet confidence. His mount was full of running while the mounts of his pursuers had very little left. In a couple of hours he would lead them by the nose due east through the run of shallow canyons and gulchs straight towards the Pecos cattle ford.

The first canyon lay about a mile ahead and a quick glance behind him told him the posse was to the rear, then his confidence received a jolt. Three more riders came over the skyline about half a mile away over to his left but only three-quarters of a mile from the canyon mouth. They seemed to size up the situation immediately and they headed towards the canyon to cut him off.

Des Willard could have turned wide enough to round the hill and keep ahead of the newcomers and the posse, but pure cussedness kept him headed straight. He hauled his Remington rifle out of the saddle-holster, and with hate in his heart, prepared to give battle.

One of the riders emerged like a bolt from the blue and Des marvelled at the speed of his mount. He sent a bullet winging towards the rider, hoping the man would swerve away, but the man was set on glory. A couple of slugs whistled past his own head and suddenly Willard was aiming in deadly earnest.

Both men bore a charmed life as their mounts closed the distance, the other riders were far behind and the battle belonged to Des and Mog Hogan. Des thrust the rifle back into the saddle-holster and rode Indian fashion, firing with his six-gun between the palomino's outstretched head and neck, then Des felt his great-hearted horse check, race on a few yards then stumble into the dust, and there was wild rage in his heart as he jumped clear and stood straddle-legged with his guns trained on the rider now almost upon him. He had a brief view of Hogan's excited face as the man's rifle swept down in line with his heart, before his guns turned the face into a bloody mass.

Even as Hogan slid out of the saddle Des

was alongside the big, black stallion, and swinging astride the animal. Without hardly checking its speed the horse thundered into the canyon.

The loss of the palomino brought out the latent savagery in Des Willard and he brought the wilful black horse around and sent it pounding back out of the canyon. He swooped low to pick up Hogan's rifle and his mount swept past, then he headed straight towards Hogan's companions. They split and fanned out wide, heading away from the canyon, the odds suddenly not to their liking.

Willard gave the stallion its head, chasing the rider farthest from the posse, and each leggy stride seemed to haul the other man back. He recognised Con Henekey at the moment the man slewed his mount around on its haunches, the animal's forelegs came down and Henekey's guns blazed. He was a fraction out, and the single shot that killed him was aimed from beneath the black's outstretched head. Willard was borne past Indian fashion as Henekey keeled over and hung suspended by one foot that had got caught up in the stirrup.

The posse had come to a stop, and Willard checked Hogan's rifle as he sent his mount into a wide turn, then suddenly he jumped clear out of the saddle, at the same time letting the long lead rein slip to the ground. The animal ran on a few paces, taking the attention of the posse while Des took careful aim before sending the bullets remaining in the magazine towards the grouped riders. He was up in a flash, and even as he was swinging back into the saddle he saw there were now two riderless horses in the posse. As he headed back for the canyon with rifle bullets whining past him he reflected that one way and another he was sure clearing the range.

As he crossed the line of the canyon mouth Des checked behind him and saw the posse was on the move again, no doubt infuriated by their casualties, but with this fireball of a horse under him he had no worries. With the very last rifle shot that was fired before he was swallowed up in his own dust the ricocheting slug buried itself into his left calf.

The shock nearly unsaddled him, but he hung on, biting his lips and grimly aware of the blood running wet and hot into his boot and knew that soon he would have to stop and stem the flow. He need not have worried, the magnificent horse kept up its speed without raising a sweat, through a series of canyons into the open country again, where he stopped over the breast of the highest ground to investigate the extent of his wound.

The top of his calf-length boot was a jagged mess and some of the leather was tangled in the gaping wound that had been torn in his calf-muscle. Des cursed Hogan's lack of foresight as he searched in the saddle-roll for bandages and he had to content himself by cutting away the top half of the boot, using his bandanna as a plug in the wound, then binding it in place with strips cut from a blanket.

Before remounting, Willard consoled himself with a cigarette, the pain from the wound was tolerable but he knew a doctor would need to attend to it mighty soon. As he rode away to the east he saw three riders spill out of the last canyon, but he was not unduly concerned. The sun had slipped behind the massive Guadaloupe Mountains and night was close at hand. He gave them a chance to sight him, then he eased his grip on the rein and his mount settled into an easy, distance-eating gallop.

During the remainder of daylight he kept heading in a straight line, always maintaining the right distance from the posse, that was now strung out in a long line abreast. When darkness fell, he gave the stallion its head for about ten minutes, then he travelled in a wide, curving run to eventually check the animals speed back farther when he considered he was properly set on the course that would bring him out on the Pecos trail. When the stars brightened he changed direction fractionally, and he reckoned that

174

with reasonable luck he should meet up with Mallory, the posse should keep on going straight for the Pecos cattle ford.

Des Willard reckoned without Slim Manning's natural ability to follow a trail and the fact that the Deputy now felt his continued existence depended entirely upon Willard's demise. Manning travelled in the wrong direction until the moon came up, then seeing he was all wrong, back-trailed and eventually picked up the sign. When he was convinced that Willard was heading over the hills for the Pecos trail, he led his men to the south-west in order to skirt the hills and so hit the Pecos trail nearer to Butane. He reckoned their mounts could make the extra distance with less effort than struggling up and down the innumerable slopes that separated them from the trail.

Willard rode through the night, smoking incessantly to take his mind off the pain from his leg that increased steadily. He was thankful that the bleeding seemed to have stopped. He had taken the route that would give him the best view of the Pecos–Butane trail between two canyons where he would have the advantage of rising ground that was pock-marked with deep folds and studded with boulders and outcrops, and about half an hour before dawn he ground-hitched his horse in a deep fold and walked the last quarter of a mile.

The terrain was rough, and with his left leg alternating between absolute numbness and pulsating pain the sweat rolled down Willard's face and body with the effort. It was not until the sun cleared the hills that he discovered how wise he had been to leave his horse behind and move into position without noise.

The man below had been slumped behind a boulder during the last minutes of moon-light but when the first fingers of light in the east heralded the sun he had emerged and stood up to peer between two jagged rocks towards the trail. Willard froze and saw the shape materialise into Creasey, one of Dainton's hired hands. There was no doubting Creasey's purpose. The man stepped back from the look-out and checked the mechanism of his rifle, then took another long look at the trail.

Time rolled on, and the sun, clear of the hills, was like a molten ball. The sweat started to roll again and Des found himself hoping the man for whom Creasey lay in wait would show up mighty soon. He saw Creasey take a drink out of a bottle and concluded the man must have waited a long time. Drink and dry-gulching did not mix, so Creasey must have anticipated a long vigil.

As Creasey replaced the bottle, Willard saw the rider emerge out of the canyon to his right, and even as he recognised Jack Mallory he realised that he and Creasey were waiting for the same man. Des watched Creasey bring his rifle to bear and follow the moving target, and his own gun was aimed to miss the man by a few inches. He just could not bring himself to put a slug into the man's back. When he killed Creasey he wanted it to be face to face.

Mallory was close when Willard saw Creasey intensify his concentration. Willard's .38 barked a split second before Creasey fired and, as Creasey spun around wild-eyed, so Mallory flung himself out of the saddle and groped for his gun.

The sudden shock had not robbed Creasey of his deadly efficiency. As he turned, he saw Willard and even before his rifle clattered to the ground his side-guns cleared leather. At this point Willard reckoned they were even and he fired to kill with a cold, clinical detachment. As Creasey disappeared from sight, Des stared through the curling gun-smoke towards Mallory and was shocked to see his old pard's face twisted into an expression of hate. Mallory's guns were out and they belched smoke. The slugs passed so close that Des felt the wind of their passing. The next one gouged a furrow in his scalp and he slumped to the ground in a heap.

Jack Mallory allowed a few minutes to slip away before he started the climb to where Willard had fallen. The past had crowded back into his mind and he remembered how close he and Des had been. It seemed incomprehensible that events should have led them to this, and that he would have the blood of his boyhood friend on his hands for ever. The fact that Willard had tried killing him from ambush did not seem to ease the sorrow that flooded him. He had a vague feeling that somewhere along the line he had taken away the prop of friendship just when it had most been needed. It took a physical effort to throw the milling thoughts into the back of his mind and to set his feet to the terraced hillside.

With his eyes riveted upon the point where Des Willard had fallen, Mallory passed Creasey's body without seeing it and he climbed upwards until he came to where Willard lay with blood seeping out from his scalp. Mallory noticed the roughly bandaged leg as he dropped to his knees beside the fallen man. His spirits rose as he felt the strong, steady pulse-beat and he was able to examine the head wound with his emotions under control. He breathed more easily when he saw that the bullet had not lodged in Willard's scalp. The furrow was deep enough but certainly not fatal.

Picking the .38 up he placed it in Willard's holster, then carefully he picked his pard up and started down the hillside. It was then he saw Creasey's legs and feet. Before he reached the point where Creasey lay stretched rigid in death, Mallory had added up the score and he was cursing himself loud and long as he stared down at the evidence. He picked up the rifle after laying Willard down. It had just been fired, then the sideguns, it was obvious that Willard had taken care of Creasey before the man could fire them.

After ensuring that Willard was lying comfortably away from the rays of the sun, Jack Mallory hurried back down the hill to the trail and, remounting his cayuse, set the animal to the slope. He found Creasey's mount easily enough but the big, black stallion that had carried Willard throughout the night took some finding, and it was only after he had studiously backtracked from where Willard had fallen did he find the animal. The horse-breeder in Mallory made him stop stock-still to study the stallion. If ever he had seen equine perfection, then the time was now. As his eyes roved over the animal with open admiration he realised he was looking at the one horse that could make for perfection in the strain he was trying to evolve. He would have been surprised to know that the mare that had foaled this superb animal had been the one he had lost four years ago and later found with the meat picked from her bones by the vultures. Hogan had held her until she had foaled and set the youngster up, then had returned her to her own range and shot her.

It was hard work under the broiling sun manhandling Creasey's body and Willard's limp weight on to the two horses and Jack Mallory was bathed in perspiration before the job was accomplished. Then with Willard's horse tethered to his own saddle cantle and Creasey's horse strong out behind, he set them moving slowly downhill to the trail. Gaining the trail, he dressed his pard's head-wound, then built himself a smoke before heading towards Butane. One thing he determined as he drew deeply on the cigarette: he would not enter Butane until nightfall when he could smuggle Willard into the Scott's house and get him the necessary medical attention.

With this decision in mind he checked back his mount's gait to little above walking speed and spun out the time to negotiate the long canyons that sheltered them from the sun's merciless heat. The wind funnelling through the narrow canyons was hot enough to have come from a furnace, but it was preferable to travelling at snail's pace under the sun.

The little cavalcade emerged from a canyon to a long run where on one side of the trail the ground fell away steeply, and the other, sharply rising side curved away, following the contour of the mountain. For a couple of miles they travelled with the trail mostly hidden behind the shoulder of the mountain, so the surprise was complete when horsemen moved out from behind a jutting, rocky outcrop and spanned the trail.

Mallory's first impulse was to go for his guns but he fought it down. Manning's bitter, black eyes staring star bright out of a face grey with alkali, told him that the posse meant business and that gunplay now might take care of a couple of men but his own death would be certain. He decided to wait his chance.

'Looks like you did a good job of work, Mallory.' Manning said icily as he rode past and pulled up alongside Willard. 'But not good enough. We'll get him strung up at the first tree we find.' Manning moved on and looked at Creasey's body. 'What happened to Creasey?' he asked.

'Bit short on speed.' Mallory was terse. 'I guess I was lucky that Willard was busy with Creasey.' It was the simple truth, but the tired riders read into his statement what he wanted them to read. 'I was toting him in to Butane so he could get tried legally and folk could see justice done properly.'

Al Cope and Seth Dyson, two of the more level-headed members of the posse, voiced their agreement but Manning rounded on them swiftly. He wanted Willard dead, and dead soon. 'We'll string him up at the next tree!' he gritted. 'You hombres saw what Willard can do last night. He killed some good men! Your pards! Nope siree! we'll take him in with his neck stretched some.'

Without further ado Manning unhitched the lead rein from Mallory's saddle-cantle and tethered it to his own. Then with complete disregard for the wounded man's comfort, he rode off ahead of the posse and Mallory.

Mallory tagged along at the back of the posse, feigning uninterest regarding Manning's intentions, and at length they rode out of the gulch, with the twisting, hill-hugging Butane trail ahead. Inevitably, a stunted oak with one straggling branch reaching out almost to the trail's edge showed up and Manning rode his horse beneath the gnarled branch. 'This'll do!' he snarled as he sent his lariat snaking over, and eager hands helped him to form the noose and make the rope secure. Without preamble, Manning led Willard's horse underneath. He turned to a couple of men. 'Prop the coyote up in the saddle, let's get him dancing on air.'

As Manning spoke, so Mallory heard the first drumming of hooves as riders approached from Butane and his hopes sank but he was not ready to count the cost. He fired one shot that sent Manning's sombrero flying and seven men swivelled to look into the menacing barrels of Mallory's guns.

Manning's dark features held a sneer. 'Just how long do you think you can keep us on the end of your guns?' The drumming hooves were more insistent and Manning's sneer deepened. 'Sounds like some more company coming to add to your problems.'

'Drop your gunbelts!' Mallory ordered. 'Either Willard gets tried in Butane or you, Manning, gets toted in dead, and one other dies with you.'

Manning dragged his eyes away from Mallory and swivelled slowly in the saddle to await the newcomers, while his posse un-buckled their gunbelts. A dozen riders burst into view and Manning's shoulders drooped as Abe Cotton held his hand aloft to bring his men to a stop.

Abe Cotton saw the way of things and his lips spread in a smile as his glance held Mallory for an instant. He motioned his men to fan out to cover the posse, then he led Des Willard's mount away. Mallory followed close, then almost in unison, the herders swung round and closed behind Mallory. Neither Manning nor the posse moved until the riders turned the bend of the trail, and there was complete absence of enthusiasm about their movements.

Chapter Eleven

'The way it stands, Miss Sheila, there's about $1,000 you can call your own, the rest belongs to the depositors.'

Ed Slade's voice carried the right degree of sorrow and his expression was that of an employee who hated to see the old firm go under. 'I guess mighty soon now a lot of folk are going to be hankering for their money, so the sooner you sign for me to realize on the bonds we hold the better.'

Sheila Scott stared hard at the ledgers Slade had brought to her as though attempting to follow the rows of neatly printed figures. 'You don't think it's possible to keep the bank going?' she asked.

Slade shook his head. 'No, ma'am. I reckon it's better to fold it up now before those bonds depreciate any. That way you come out of it with something. A run of bad luck and you'll end up owing money.'

Sheila nodded her head slowly. 'And what about you?' she asked. 'What will you do?'

The little teller's eyes widened and his face took on an expression of open frankness. 'Well, I've been mighty careful over the years, Miss Sheila,' he said smoothly. 'So I

184

guess I may start up in a small way on my own.'

'A bank, you mean?'

'Yeah, ma'am. I reckon it's the only business I know. You see, I'd start up only taking what I could handle and taking my own investment chances.' Slade's head wagged from side to side in sorrow as he continued. 'I sure wish I had your father's know-how, he'd have gotten over the bad run if that coyote Willard hadn't killed him.'

Sheila's eyes glistened a bit as his words brought her loss back to her and Slade hastened to apologise for mentioning her father's death, but he had done what he had intended to do – conveyed to her that he was unequal to the task of carrying on the bank as it stood for her.

'Perhaps you'll leave the papers for me to sign,' Sheila said after she had composed herself. 'The ledgers too; maybe I'll be able to understand them better if I look at them on my own.'

Slade nodded and stood up. 'I guess tomorrow will do, Miss Sheila,' he said. 'You stay there, ma'am. I'll see myself out.'

Sheila Scott waited for the front door to close behind Ed Slade, then she went straight through to the inner room to where Seth Dormer stood in front of the open fireplace with a glass of bourbon in his hands. 'You were right, Mr Dormer,' she said. 'He wants me to sign so that the bonds still held can be sold to pay back the investors. He's left the papers and ledgers with me until tomorrow.'

Dormer smiled and nodded his satisfaction. 'Couldn't be better,' he remarked. 'I guess it won't be long before young Mallory hits town and if he brings back the information I wanted, then it'll be mighty handy to have those ledgers to hand.'

Sheila coloured a little as she thought of Jack Mallory. She wanted him back from Pecos but not for the same reason as Dormer. The horse-trader's kind eyes were on her as the colour rose and she moved to the doorway quickly. 'I'll take my turn with Robins,' she said. 'Maybe Sal will get herself some rest then. You should get some rest too,' she added.

'I'll stretch my length on the settle for a while,' Dormer replied. 'Then I'll make the final arrangements for this afternoon.'

The arrangements were for the interment of Ezra Scott, and Sheila flashed him a look of gratitude before leaving him to his own devices. Dormer refilled his glass and stretched out on the settle. There was an air of contentment about him as he mulled things over. His only worry had been that Willard would manage to keep ahead of the posse throughout the night and as the morning rolled on and on it seemed more and more certain that Willard had in fact succeeded. If the posse had caught up with their quarry, then they would have lost no time in hitting town to celebrate their success. He reckoned now that Amos Cotton would have things under control.

Ed Slade turned into the Maverick saloon and made his way to his usual table. Hubert Dainton turned away from Tyler, who had been helping him prop the bar up, and grasping his bottle of bourbon, reached for the glasses Con Sullivan slid across the bar before crossing to join Slade. The two men drank in silence a long time and Tyler watching, wondered again just what drew his boss and Slade together.

'By tomorrow I reckon we'll have everything settled up, Hubert,' Slade said quickly. 'She's good and ready to sign.' Dainton smiled but there was a guarded expression about his eyes.

'I'd be a mite happier if Nolan hadn't got himself wiped out,' he muttered. 'Dormer's not going to believe that Nolan had a personal grudge and he'll likely stay around to find out who set Nolan after him.' Slade shrugged his shoulders, then helped himself to a cigar out of his vest pocket. 'Maybe Dormer will add things up to the right score but he can't prove anything.' Slade paused to get his cigar going properly. 'Just as long as we sit tight, no amount of prodding is going to help him, so, sooner or later, he's gonna light out after that horse herd of his.'

'No doubt you're right,' Dainton said at length, but his doubts persisted. Creasey should have been back long ago with the chore of killing Mallory completed, and his continued absence pointed only too patently to the failure of his mission. It was all right for Slade to be philosophical but Nolan and Creasey led automatically to Hubert Dainton. For the first time Dainton gave weighty consideration to his little companion's facility for keeping outside of things. He knew Slade to be a cold-blooded killer and equal to any man in the ability to plan wholesale slaughter, but there was nothing that could tie Slade to him irrevocably. Dainton downed a big gulp of bourbon to help swallow the unpalatable truth that, if a showdown came, Slade would still survive to reap the rewards while he would go under.

Slade must have picked up Dainton's thoughts and when Dainton next looked at him there was a light of mockery in the little man's eyes. 'Take it easy, Hubert,' Slade said smoothly. 'The game's nearly won.'

Dainton's reply was forestalled by the sudden burst of yelling in the street and the sound of horsemen. The other customers in the saloon crowded out on to the sidewalk and Dainton followed quickly. He pushed his way to the sidewalk rail and his face was a study as he took in the procession of horsemen. Slade eased beside him and after a quick glance returned to the saloon. Dainton's eyes skimmed away hastily from Creasey's prone figure. Creasey was very dead. They rested briefly on Willard and a curse slipped from his lips when it became apparent the man was still alive.

The crowd gathered quickly as the party of horsemen stopped outside the jailhouse, and excitement ran high as men shouted to one another that Willard was caught. From the fringe of the crowd came the first lynching call and in moments loud-throated yells were clamouring to have Willard strung up. Dainton's spirits rose considerably and he shouted as loud as anyone.

The ranks around Willard tightened as Dormer's men bunched close and the press of townsfolk fell away when they found themselves looking into the barrels of the horse-herders' guns. Abe Cotton, sitting tall in the saddle and looking every inch the Scout with his long hair, pointed beard and fringed buckskin coat, raised his hand for silence and, after a couple of moments, the shouting stopped.

'If you hombres are really set on a lynching, then I guess that's the way it'll be.' He paused not so much for effect but to ensure they were listening. 'The only trouble is that we don't go along with lynching and we aim to stop it if we can. If you fellers persist, then a lot of folk are going to die. If you let Willard get tried legally by a jury, then only the guilty's going to die. The choice is yours, but right from now anybody who shouts for a lynching will get a bullet in his windpipe.'

There was a sudden lack of enthusiasm and the men on the sidewalks who had shouted loudest relapsed into silence, those of the crowd who were nearest to the rock-steady guns held by the calm, efficient looking trail-herders, were only too ready to concede that Abe Cotton spoke good sense. Their only worry was that some goddarned fools at the back would start something, leaving them to soak up the first fusillade of lead.

Slim Manning tried to regain some of his lost authority by forcing his mount through the crowd and stopping in front of Cotton. 'There'll be no lynching,' he shouted. 'Just hand over the prisoner and we'll get him locked up where he'll be safe.'

Cotton's loud laugh brought cold fury to Manning's eyes but the Deputy held himself in check.

'You can go to Hades, Manning! When the doc says Willard is good and ready to stand trial we'll produce him, but not before. Moreover, anyone trying to get to him before the trial will earn himself a ride to Boot Hill.'

Manning swung round in the saddle and looked around the townsfolk. His glance touched on Hubert Dainton but the rancher's expression was non-committal and the Deputy addressed himself to the crowd. 'Are you hombres gonna stand by and let these trail-herders take over the running of your town?'

There was a long period of silence, broken only by the fidgeting of tired horses. Manning assumed a long-suffering look as he stared around the townsfolk again but, in reality, he was relieved to have received no support against Cotton and his men. He was now at liberty to publicly renounce his appointment and leave town, and his instinct told him this was his best course. With a flamboyant gesture he unfastened the star from his vest and tossed it to the crowd. 'I guess that lets me out, then,' he shouted. 'I reckon I'll find me a town where folk carry a bit more sand.'

'You're not going any place, Manning! You're staying right here till after the trial.' Cotton's voice was authoritative.

'There's nothing to keep me here if I'm not allowed to do my job,' Manning countered.

'That's your mistake, Manning. I reckon these smoke-poles will keep you in town.' As he spoke, Cotton nodded to a couple of his men and they moved alongside the Deputy. One of them stuck his gun-barrel into Manning's back while the other disarmed the Deputy, then the townsfolk were treated to the sight of their former lawman being ordered off his cayuse and marched into his own jail. A couple more of the horse-herders dismounted and took up positions outside the jail, then Abe Cotton gave the signal to get moving. The crowd fell away, leaving a clear path for the riders, and they watched Cotton and his men stop outside the Scotts' house, then carry Willard inside. Jack Mallory followed. The attention of the crowd switched to Creasey's body but there was no one to tell them how Creasey came to be dead. It palled as a spectacle, and Seth Dyson and Al Cope led the horse bearing the burden away to the funeral-parlour.

Hubert Dainton's sense of unease increased as the crowd dissolved. On the surface nothing had changed, the cards were still stacked against Des Willard and trial by jury should still result in him being hanged. Judge Carter was back and he had never been known to miss up on a hanging chance. Despite all this, Dainton had the feeling that before long the attentions of Dormer and his men would be directed towards himself. He needed shoring up and as he turned to re-enter the Maverick he dispatched Tyler to the Box Q with explicit instructions to bring in enough men to outnumber the horse-herders. When Dainton resumed his seat at the table, Ed Slade stood up.

'Few things I want to see to at the bank,' he murmured. 'Then I guess it'll be time to pay my last respects to my old boss.'

Dainton was a bit nonplussed by Slade's sudden departure. There were things he wanted to talk about, like the possibility of Manning blowing the gaff about Suter's killing and various other points. He took a few quick drinks, then felt more equal to attacking the problem on his own. Manning presented a real threat to him. The man had gall enough to stand pressures if his own neck was at stake but Dainton could not imagine him passing up a chance to clear himself at someone else's expense. It took the best part of a bottle of bourbon to restore Dainton's confidence, but, at length, when he made his way to the hotel section to get spruced up for Ezra Scott's interment, he had recovered some of his old poise. Come nightfall and he would have his entire roughneck crew at his side, so he reckoned that he would be able to handle anything that cropped up.

After the funeral, Dainton concluded that his earlier fears had been groundless. There had been no semblance of animosity on the parts of Dormer or Mallory during the short time they had been thrown together. Neither man seemed to saddle Dainton with any responsibility for the actions of Nolan and Creasey and when he heard from Al Cope that Mallory had been responsible for

Willard's head wound, then it seemed to Dainton his troubles were over and it appeared that the horse-herders were, after all, only concerned with the technicalities of the law. If he had any fleeting worries about Manning they were put at rest when the ex-Deputy made an appearance just after sundown. The two men had a couple of drinks together and Manning's words started Dainton counting chickens again.

'The way those herders are talking, they're as set on a hanging as much as anyone; it seems they want the fun of a trial as well. Dormer told 'em to let me go, providing I did my job as Deputy an' rustled up a jury ready for the trial. He reckons Willard should be ready to face up to things by tomorrow.'

'When you get around to finding the jury don't forget Kershawe, he's mighty riled about Willard rubbing out his sidekick Smeaton.'

'He's blamed lucky he didn't get the same medicine,' Manning growled. 'We only showed up in time to save his skin. As it was, Willard killed Hogan and Levin. Just after we hit town Cronin and Lear headed out to bury 'em.' Manning paused to light himself a cigarette. 'Don't worry any, I'll get a jury that'll fix Willard up good.'

The news of the trial having been set for the next day sent a thrill of excitement through the town and the saloons bulged with humanity, all intent upon celebrating the hanging before the event. Willard's guilt was a foregone conclusion, and with Judge Carter to prompt what in any case would be a hostile jury, his chances of escaping the noose could be discounted. By midnight, Dainton's outfit swelled the ranks in the Maverick where also Dormer's crew of trail-herders congregated, so Hubert Dainton's fears completely evaporated as the night wore on and the herders expressed vociferous belief in rapid justice for proven killers.

Very few men went to bed that night in Butane. Most of them kept up the celebrations until an hour or so before sun-up and they slept in the saloons, slumped across tables until the Alpine Stage thundered out of town to the accompaniment of hoarse yells from the driver, who felt sore at having to miss the fun. The drinking started up again at that point and some of the more blood-thirsty strolled out into the sunlight to study the tree that would have to take Willard's weight.

Men breakfasted hurriedly, then mindful of the size of the courthouse, drifted in twos and threes to make sure of seats. There was a long wait ahead of them but they considered the entertainment would be worth the trouble. Once inside the court-house they ran the gauntlet of Abe Cotton and three other herders, who relieved them of their gunbelts and, although some men made token protests, the iron resolve on the faces of the herders and Abe Cotton's twin guns convinced them it was smart to play along. Ringed around the courthouse were a few more of Dormer's men, all armed. It seemed that Dormer was determined to run things properly.

By about nine o'clock every available seat was taken and a crowd milled around outside, waiting for the judge and the prisoner to show up. The jury trooped inside headed by Slim Manning and, if Willard's hopes of survival had been entirely in their hands, then he might just as well have forgone the farce of a trial. Hank Kershawe was as loud-mouthed as ever and was busy hammering home Willard's guilt to his fellow jurors, even as he pushed his way through the pressing crowd.

Just before ten o'clock, the Scotts' door opened and Willard emerged, white-faced, with his head heavily bandaged. Dormer, Mallory and Doc Colehan were at his side, with Dormer and Mallory giving him some support for his game leg. Briefly, the faces of Sal Dormer and Sheila Scott showed in the doorway, then the door slammed and the prisoner was on his way to face trial. Two more of Dormer's men walked ahead of the bunch and their hands were held ominously close to the butts of their low-slung guns.

The crowd fell away, leaving space enough on the sidewalk for the grim-faced group, and on no side was any sympathy shown for the wounded prisoner. Once Willard and his escort entered the courthouse, the crowd rushed for the tree of execution. They might be missing the fun in the courthouse but they intended to be right in the middle of the pay-off.

Judge Carter stomped his bombastic, officious way along the sidewalk just behind Dainton, Ed Slade and Tyler to the accompaniment of the first cheer he had ever known. Then the courthouse doors were closed and the trial was under way.

The judge had a reputation for hustling a trial along and he had no intention of allowing this one to nibble into his drinking time. First Manning gave his evidence, then Dainton, in an almost apologetic manner, as though mindful of the fact Willard was his nephew. When Tyler started in to say the same piece Carter rapped his desk with his hammer impatiently. 'There's no call to say the whole durned thing again,' he bellowed. 'Just say "yes" or "no" to what the other two said.'

Tyler shrugged his shoulders and nodded. 'Yeah! It happened like they said,' he said loudly.

Judge Carter turned to the jury and wagged his forefinger at them. 'You've got that clear. Witnesses say Willard fired two shots at Sheriff Suter, one grazed his scalp and the other went through his heart.'

'Sure, Judge,' Hank Kershawe growled. 'It's plain enough to us.'

Carter's malevolent eyes switched to Willard, who stood between Dormer and Mallory in the witness-box. 'If you've got anything to say, get it said.'

Willard's bitter glance swept around the courthouse and back to Judge Carter. 'I've got plenty to say but I guess you ain't got the time to listen,' he said quietly.

Judge Carter brushed the remark aside with his customary brusqueness. 'All you've got to say is that you did or didn't kill Suter.'

'In that case I didn't kill him, like I've said before, I only fired one shot an' that creased Suter's skull.'

Carter's reply was a short laugh. He pointed to the three figures in the front row. 'There are three witnesses that say different, Willard,' he bellowed. 'Three witnesses who are known solid citizens.'

'That's right enough, Judge,' Slim Manning put in. 'Another thing is the doc dug a .38 slug out of Sheriff Suter and we all know Willard always toted 38s.'

'Maybe the doc should dig again into Suter's body,' Des Willard said in a clear voice, and it was noticeable that the witnesses in the front row sat up, stiffly attentive. 'It

198

could be he'd find a slug of another calibre that did the damage.'

The Judge did not even entertain that suggestion and he extracted a cigar from his vest pocket and, after snipping off the end, inspected it prior to lighting up. This was his normal procedure before winding up a case. 'If you've got nothing more to say, Willard, I guess the jury can make up their minds.'

'Maybe Willard's run out of words, Judge, but I've got a few questions to ask the witnesses, just so that we get things clear,' Seth Dormer broke in. A spasm of annoyance ran across Carter's face but he had no intention of crossing Dormer. He had discovered that Dormer had some very influential friends who held the keys to better circuits than Butane County. He jammed the cigar back into his vest pocket and nodded his agreement. The three witnesses tried to look helpful as they awaited the Deputy US Marshal's questions.

'It seems mighty strange to me that Willard was able to get two shots at Sheriff Suter yet none of you hombres went for the hardware.' Dormer glanced from Slim Manning to Hubert Dainton and Tyler, but their expressions gave nothing away. 'There were two other trigger-happy punchers siding you too – Nolan and Creasey – and those two sure liked spraying plenty of lead when the chips were down!'

'Willard had his guns trained on us when we rounded the bend, Dormer,' Slim Manning snarled. 'There was no sense in bucking those odds. We all knew Willard's ability with six-guns. Mebbe from an even start things would have been different.'

Judge Carter rapped his desk angrily. 'If that's the sort of questions you're going to ask, Dormer, then by my book it's a waste of time.'

Seth Dormer did not even bother to look at the judge. There was a grim smile on his face as he turned his attention to Ed Slade. 'I guess we've proved that Willard's no slouch with the shooting irons,' he said quietly. 'We're lucky enough to have witnesses for the killing of Suter but the killing of Ezra Scott is different. The proof here that Willard killed him is the .38 slug that was dug out of Scott's body. This killing was a mighty sad blow to this town,' Dormer went on. 'Ezra Scott was well liked and I guess you'd say, Mr Slade, that the killing happened at just about the worst time for the bank. Just so the jury will understand, maybe you'll tell 'em how the bank stands.'

'Yeah, sure.' Ed Slade was lulled by Dormer's apparent acceptance of Willard's guilt. 'Ezra Scott had been speculating some and the luck had gone against him. At the time he got killed the assets just about covered the depositors' money.'

Dormer turned first to the judge, then to the jury. 'You heard that. The bank was going downhill.'

'Dormer!' Judge Carter roared. 'What in tarnation has the assets of the bank got to do with Willard?'

'Just this, Judge.' Dormer's face was set in hard lines and his eyes spat fire. 'If Willard killed Ezra Scott he did it for small change. If he didn't, then someone else did for a quarter of a million dollars.'

It took a long time for the significance of Dormer's remark to sink in, then suddenly the atmosphere in the courthouse was tense and every eye was on Dormer. Slade's eyes were bird-bright and Hubert Dainton's face had lost its general expression of bonhomie.

Dormer extracted a sheaf of papers out of his vest pocket and placed them on Judge Carter's table. 'I happen to be a director of the Chase National Bank and that's the reply from the Secretary to some questions I sent him. According to this, Butane's bank is a mighty healthy concern and your figures, Mr Slade, don't make sense.'

Ed Slade shrugged his shoulders and his smile looked genuine. 'I'm sure glad to hear it, Mr Dormer,' he said. 'I guess my figures were on account of what Ezra Scott told me. It looks like he had his own reasons for showing he was near bust.'

Dormer shook his head. 'That's not so,

Slade. Your books are no more than a string of lies, an' if Miss Scott had signed the paper you left with her you'd have taken over that quarter of a million dollars I mentioned.'

Ed Slade stood up slowly and there was bitterness on his face. 'You've got no call to say that, Dormer!' he exclaimed.

'I'll say more, Slade.' Dormer cut in. 'I'll say you killed Ezra Scott so's you could lay your hands on the bank's assets.'

Ed Slade looked around the courthouse, an expression of bewildered hopelessness on his face. 'You're loco, Dormer. Plumb loco. You know durned well that Willard killed him, like you said the doc took a .38 slug out of Scott.'

'I've got a witness who says you've toted a .38.'

'Then he's a liar.' Ed Slade shouted. 'You tell me who it is and I'll tell him he's a god-durned liar.'

'Sure.' As Dormer spoke he fingered out of his pocket the misshapen slug that Willard had removed from the little Box Q cook. He held it up between thumb and forefinger. 'This is the .38 slug that was dug out of the witness, Slade, and the witness says you shot him. He's sure told me a lot more interesting things too, like how he tampered with the evidence an' planted a slug in Suter's corpse so as to keep suspicion away from Dainton, his sidekicks an' that so-called Deputy, Manning.' Dormer paused to let his words sink in.

Judge Carter was stupefied and the jury, handpicked by Manning to a man were aghast at the change in proceedings. All around the courthouse men were straining forward to catch Dormer's every word. Hubert Dainton, Manning and Tyler were all suddenly pale and strained about the eyes, while Ed Slade was staring at the .38 slug as though mesmerised.

'Yeah, we brought Squinty Robins back to life, Slade, after you'd plugged him and sent him out of town on his horse, and he's good and ready to say his piece. Nolan told me plenty, too, before he passed out, like who killed Jeff Willard.' Dormer turned briefly to ensure that Judge Carter was taking proper note, then with a swift fluid movement he drew one of his guns and tossed it to the smiling Willard.

The move was calculated and had the desired effect. Dormer's deep foresight had prompted him to instruct his men at the courthouse door to allow Dainton's hands and the witnesses to keep their side-arms, for he knew that, faced with the evidence, they would react in the manner that would prove conclusively Willard's innocence. Townsfolk hurled themselves to the floor as men clawed for their shooting-irons and the courthouse erupted as guns blasted.

Long after the firing had ceased, the building seemed to reverberate with noise, and the gunsmoke hung like a pall over the grim-faced men who surveyed the carnage wrought by their guns. The edge had been with Dormer, Mallory and Willard, and the sprawled figures of Slade, Dainton and Tyler tangled amidst the upset chairs bore testimony to the fact. Dormer's herders, lined around the wall of the building, had taken care of Dainton's men, and only two of their number, standing with hands aloft, escaped the reckoning.

Slowly the townsfolk came up off the floor and took stock of things, but before the tension slipped away from them Dormer held his hands up for silence. Judge Carter emerged slowly and the jury got back into their places.

'I guess you all heard the way of things,' Dormer said in a loud voice. 'And you all know now that Des Willard never was guilty of any crime. I guess the court had better complete its job and take the brand of killer from him.'

Judge Carter took over with a vengeance. Although an advocate of rough-and-ready justice he preferred to leave the details of dispatch to others while he screened himself behind a saloon partition, and fortified himself with strong spirit. On this occasion he had been involved and some of the stray lead had missed him narrowly. He hammered the desk and glared at the jury. 'Let me hear your verdict of not guilty,' he bawled.

'Not guilty!' They spoke up to a man. There were no favours coming their way ever again from Dainton and they all knew how to swim with the tide.

'Case dismissed!' Carter shouted. Then as the townsfolk found their voices he rushed headlong out of the courthouse, away from the sight and smell of blood and gunsmoke, leaving the crowd surging to congratulate the suave Dormer and the two pards, Des Willard and Jack Mallory.

Even as he considered the fickleness of the crowd, the bitterness went out of Des Willard and he did not spurn the hands that shook his own. The crowd moved aside to let him and Mallory through and, as the pards neared the door, the noise outside told them the news had broken. They came out on to the sidewalk and the street was thick with people sweating it out under the boiling sun.

Neither Mallory nor Willard noticed the crowd or heeded the shouted questions that gave way to cheers. They had eyes only for the two girls now drawn away from the edge of the crowd and nothing diverted them as they pushed their way through the yelling townsfolk until at last they were clear. Then with Sal to aid him, Des Willard walked on down the street a free man. Mallory and Sheila followed close behind, hands clasped tightly.

Seth Dormer turned to Abe Cotton, who stood beside him watching. 'Looks like you'll have to push on with the herd, Abe, seems I'm going to be busy organising a couple of weddings.'

'Ugh! Weddings!' Cotton snorted. 'Well, maybe that's something you can handle on your lonesome.'

The publishers hope that this book has given you enjoyable reading. Large Print Books are especially designed to be as easy to see and hold as possible. If you wish a complete list of our books please ask at your local library or write directly to:

Dales Large Print Books
Magna House, Long Preston,
Skipton, North Yorkshire.
BD23 4ND